BY PARKER FILLMORE
CZECHOSLOVAK FAIRY TALES
THE SHOEMAKER'S APRON
Illustrated by Jan Matulka

THE
LAUGHING PRINCE

A Book of Jugoslav Fairy Tales and Folk Tales

BY

PARKER FILLMORE

WITH ILLUSTRATIONS AND DECORATIONS

BY

JAY VAN EVEREN

NEW YORK
HARCOURT, BRACE AND COMPANY

PRINTED IN THE UNITED STATES OF AMERICA

TO
BUTTON

NOTE

In calling this *A Book of Jugoslav Fairy Tales and Folk Tales* I have used the word Jugoslav in its literal sense of Southern Slav. The Bulgars are just as truly Southern Slavs as the Serbs or Croats or any other of the Slav peoples now included within the state of Jugoslavia. Moreover in this case it would be particularly difficult to make the literary boundaries conform strictly to the political boundaries since much the same stories and folk tales are current among all these Slav peoples of the Balkan Peninsula. The special student taking the variants of the same story might discover special differences that would mark each variant as the product of some one locality. The work of such a student would have philological and ethnological value but not a very strong appeal to the general reader. My appeal is first of all to the general reader—to the child who loves fairy tales and to the adult who loves them. I hope they will both find these stories entertaining and amusing quite aside from any interest in their source.

Yet these tales as presented do give the reader a true idea of the amazing vigor and the artistic inventiveness of the Jugoslav imagination, and also of the various influences, Oriental and Northern as well as Slavic, which have made that imagination what it is to-day. Here are gay picaresque tales of adventure—how they go on and on and on!—charming little stories of sentiment, a few folk tales of stark simplicity and grim humor, one story showing a superficial Turkish influence, and one spiritual allegory as deep and moving as anything in the Russian.

The renderings in every case are my own and are not in any sense translations. I have taken the old stories and retold them in a new language. To do them justice in this new language I have found it necessary to present them with a new selection of detail and with an occasional shifting of emphasis. I do not mean by this that I have invented detail in any unwarranted fashion. I haven't had to for any folk tale, however bald, contains all sorts of things by implication. The true story teller, it seems to me, is he who is able to grasp these implications and turn them to his own use.

I must confess that the setting in which I have placed the famous old Serbian nonsense story, *In my young days when I was an old, old man,* is my own invention. The nonsense story needs a setting and as it chanced I had one ready as I have long wanted to tell the world what was back of the determination of that princess who refused to eat until some one had made her laugh.

So far as I know most of these stories are not familiar to English readers—certainly not in this form. Madame Mijatovich uses one of them in her *Serbian Fairy Tales,* but I make no apology for offering a sprightlier version. Nor do I apologize for presenting any stories that may have been included somewhere among the indifferent translations to which Andrew Lang lent his name.

I am of course deeply indebted to the various people who told me these stories in the first place and to many scholarly folklorists, Jugoslav, Czechoslovak, Bulgarian, German, and English whose books and reports I have studied.

Decoration Day, 1921.   P. F.

CONTENTS

ix

THE LAUGHING PRINCE

The Story of the Boy Who Could Talk Nonsense

THE LAUGHING PRINCE

THERE was once a farmer who had three sons and one little daughter. The eldest son was a studious boy who learned so much out of books that the farmer said:

"We must send Mihailo to school and make a priest of him."

The second boy was a trader. Whatever you had he would get it from you by offering you something else for it. And always what he gave you was worth less than what you gave him.

"Jakov will make a fine peddler," the farmer said. "He's industrious and sharp and some day he will probably be a rich man."

But Stefan, the farmer's youngest son, had no special talent and because he didn't spend all his time with his nose in a book and because he never made the best of a bargain his brothers scorned him. Militza, his little sister, loved him dearly for he was kind and jolly and in the evening he was always ready to tell her stories and play with her. But the farmer, of course, listened to the older brothers.

3

"I don't know about poor Stefan," he used to say. "He's a good boy but he talks nonsense. I suppose he'll have to stay on the farm and work."

Now the truth is the farm was a fine place for Stefan for he was strong and lusty and he liked to plow and harvest and he had a wonderful way with the animals. He talked to them as if they were human beings and the horses all whinnied when he came near, and the cows rubbed their soft noses against his shoulder, and as for the pigs—they loved him so much that whenever they saw him they used to run squealing between his legs.

"Stefan is nothing but a farmer!" Mihailo used to say as though being a farmer was something to be ashamed of.

And Jakov said:

"If the village people could see the pigs following him about, how they'd laugh at him! I hope when I go to the village to live he won't be visiting me all the time!"

Another thing the older brothers couldn't understand about Stefan was why he was always laughing and joking. He did the work of two men but whether he was working or resting you could always hear him cracking his merry jokes and laughing his jolly laugh.

" I think he's foolish! " Mihailo said.

Jakov hoped that the village people wouldn't hear about his carryings on.

" They'd laugh at him," he said, " and they'd laugh at us, too, because we're his brothers."

But Stefan didn't care. The more they frowned at him, the louder he laughed, and in spite of their dark looks he kept on cracking his merry jokes and talking nonsense. And every evening after supper his little sister, Militza, clapped her hands and cried:

" Now, Stefan, tell me a story! Tell me a story! "

" Father," Mihailo would say, " you ought to make him keep quiet! He's foolish and all he does is fill Militza's head with nonsense! "

This always made Militza very indignant and she would stamp her little foot and say:

" He isn't foolish! He knows more than any one! And he can do more things than any one else and he's the handsomest brother in the world! "

You see Militza loved Stefan dearly and when you love a person of course you think that person is wonderful. But the father supposed that Mihailo must be right for Mihailo studied in books. So he shook his head and sighed every time he thought of Stefan.

Now the kingdom in which the three brothers lived

was ruled over by a great Tsar who had an only daughter. In disappointment that he had no son, the Tsar was having his daughter brought up as though she were a boy. He sent all over the world for tutors and teachers and had the poor girl taught statecraft and law and philosophy and all the other things that the heir to the throne ought to know.

The Princess because she was an obedient girl and because she loved her father tried to spend all her time in study. But the dry old scholars whom the Tsar employed as teachers were not amusing companions for a young girl and the first lady-in-waiting who was in constant attendance was scarcely any better for she, too, was old and thin and very prim.

If the poor little Princess between her geography lesson and her arithmetic lesson would peep for a moment into a mirror, the first lady-in-waiting would tap her arm reprovingly and say:

"My dear, vanity is not becoming in a princess!"

One day the little Princess lost her temper and answered sharply:

"But I'm a girl even if I am a princess and I love to look in mirrors and I love to make myself pretty and I'd love to go to a ball every night of my life and dance with handsome young men!"

"You talk like the daughter of a farmer!" the first lady-in-waiting said.

Then the Princess, because she lost her temper still further, said something she should not have said.

"I wish I were the daughter of a farmer!" she declared. "Then I could wear pretty ribbons and go dancing and the boys would come courting me! As it is I have to spend all my time with funny old men and silly old women!"

Now even if her tutors and teachers were funny looking old men, even if the first lady-in-waiting was a silly old woman, the Princess should not have said so. It hurt the feelings of the first lady-in-waiting and made her angry and she ran off to the Tsar at once and complained most bitterly.

"Is this my reward after all my years of loving service to your daughter?" she asked. "It is true that I've grown old and thin looking after her manners and now she calls me a silly old woman! And all the learned wise men and scholars that you have gathered from the far corners of the earth—she points her finger at them and calls them funny old men!"

The fact is they were funny looking, most of them, but yet the first lady-in-waiting was right: the Princess should not have said so.

"And think of her ingratitude to yourself, O Tsar!"
the first lady-in-waiting continued. "You plan to make
her the heir to your throne and yet she says she wishes
she were a farmer's daughter so that she could deck
herself out in ribbons and have the boys come courting
her! A nice thing for a princess to say!"

The Tsar when he heard this fell into an awful rage.
(The truth is whatever temper the Princess had she inherited direct from her father.)

"Wow! Wow!" he roared, just that way. "Send
the Princess to me at once. I'll soon have her singing
another tune!"

So the first lady-in-waiting sent the Princess to her
father and as soon as he saw her he began roaring again
and saying:

"Wow! Wow! What do you mean—funny old men
and silly old women?"

Now whenever the Tsar began roaring and saying,
"Wow! Wow!" the Princess always stiffened, and instead of being the sweet and obedient daughter she
usually was she became obstinate. Her pretty eyes
would flash and her soft pretty face would harden and
people would whisper: "Mercy on us, how much she
looks like her father!"

"That's just what I mean!" the Princess said.

" They're a lot of funny old men and silly old women
and I'm tired of them! I want to be amused! I want
to laugh! "

" Wow! Wow! Wow! " roared the Tsar. " A fine
princess you are! Go straight back to the schoolroom
and behave yourself! "

So the little Princess marched out of the throne room
holding her head very high and looking so much like
the Tsar that the first lady-in-waiting was positively
frightened.

The Princess went back to the schoolroom but she
did not behave herself. She was really very naughty.
When the poor man who knew more than anybody in
the world about the influence of the stars upon the
destinies of nations came to give her a lesson, she threw
his book out the window. When the superannuated old
general who was teaching her military manœuvers offered her a diagram on which the enemy was repre-
sented by a series of black dots and our soldiers by a
series of red dots, she took the paper and tore it in
two. And worst of all when the old scholar who was
teaching her Turkish—for a princess must be able to
speak all languages—dropped his horn spectacles on
the floor, she deliberately stepped on them and broke
them.

When the Tsar heard all these things he just *wow-wowed* something terrible.

"Lock that young woman in her chamber!" he ordered. "Feed her on bread and water until she's ready to apologize!"

But the Princess, far from being frightened by this treatment, calmly announced:

"I won't eat even your old bread and water until you send me some one who will make me laugh!"

Now this frightened the Tsar because he knew how obstinate the Princess could be on occasions. (He ought to know, too, for the Princess had that streak of obstinacy direct from himself.)

"This will never do!" he said.

He hurried to the Princess's chamber. He found her in bed with her pretty hair spread out on the pillow like a golden fan.

"My dear," the Tsar said, "I was joking. You don't have to eat only bread and water. You may have anything you want."

"Thank you," the Princess said, "but I'll never eat another bite of anything until you send me some one who will make me laugh. I'm tired of living in this gloomy old castle with a lot of old men and old women who do nothing but instruct me and with a father

who always loses his temper and says, ' Wow!
Wow! ' "

" But it's a beautiful castle! " the poor Tsar said.
" And I'm sure we're all doing our very best to educate
you! "

" But I want to be amused as well as educated! "
the little Princess said. And then, because she felt she
was going to cry, she turned her face to the wall and
wouldn't say another word.

What was the Tsar to do? He called together his
councilors and asked them how was the Princess to
be made to laugh. The councilors were wise about
state matters but not one of them could suggest a
means of amusing the Princess. The Master of Ceremonies did indeed begin to say something about a
nice young man but instantly the Tsar roared out
such a wrathful, " Wow! Wow! " that the Master
of Ceremonies coughed and pretended he hadn't
spoken.

Then the Tsar called together the scholars and the
teachers and the first lady-in-waiting. He glared at
them savagely and roared:

" Wow! Wow! A nice lot you are! I put you in
charge of my daughter and not one of you has sense
enough to know that the poor child needs a little amuse-

ment! I have a good mind to have you all thrown
into the dungeon!"

"But, Your Majesty," quavered one poor old
scholar, "I was not employed as a buffoon but as a
teacher of astrology!"

"And I," another said, "as a teacher of languages!"

"And I as a teacher of philosophy!"

"Silence!" roared the Tsar. "Between you all you
have about killed my poor child! Now I ask you: With
all your learning doesn't one of you know how to make
a young girl laugh?"

Apparently not one of them did, for no one answered.

"Not even you?" the Tsar said, looking at the first
lady-in-waiting.

"When you called me to Court," the first lady-in-
waiting answered, drawing herself up in a most refined
manner, "you said you wished me to teach your daughter etiquette. As you said nothing about amusement,
quite naturally I confined myself to the subject of be-
havior. If I do say it myself, no one has ever been
more devoted to duty than I. I am constantly saying
to her: 'That isn't the way a princess should act!' In
fact for years there has hardly been a moment in the
day when I haven't corrected her for something!"

" Poor child! " groaned the Tsar. " No wonder she wants a change! Oh, what fools you all are in spite of your learning! Don't you know that a young girl is a young girl even if she is a Princess! "

Well, the scholars weren't any more help to the Tsar than the councilors, and finally in desperation he sent heralds through the land to announce that to any one who could make the Princess laugh he would give three bags of gold.

Three bags of gold don't grow on the bushes every day and instantly all the youths and men and old men who had stories that their sweethearts and their wives and their daughters laughed at hurried to the castle.

One by one they were admitted to the Princess's chamber. They entered hopefully but when they saw the Tsar sitting at one side of the door muttering, " Wow! Wow! " in his beard, and the old first lady-in-waiting at the other side of the door watching them scornfully, and the Princess herself in bed with her lovely hair spread out like a golden fan on the pillow, they forgot their funny stories and hemmed and hawed and stammered and had finally, one after another, to be turned out in disgrace.

One day went by and two and three and still the Princess refused to eat. In despair the Tsar sent out

his heralds again. This time he said that to any one
who would make the Princess laugh he would give the
Princess's hand in marriage and make him joint heir
to the kingdom.

"I had expected to wed her to the son of some great
Tsar," he sighed, "but I'd rather marry her to a farmer
than see her die of starvation!"

The heralds rode far and wide until every one, even
the people on the most distant farms, had heard of the
Tsar's offer.

"I won't try again," said Mihailo, the oldest son of
the farmer I've already told you about. "When I
went there the day before yesterday I began telling
her a funny story out of my Latin book but instead of
laughing she said: 'Oh, send him away!' So now she'll
have to starve to death for all of me!"

"Me, too!" said Jakov, the second son. "When I
tried to tell her that funny story of how I traded the
moldy oats for the old widow's fat pig, instead of laughing she looked me straight in the face and said:
'Cheat!'"

"Stefan ought to go," Mihailo suggested. "Maybe
she'd laugh at him! Everybody else does!"

He spoke sneeringly but Stefan only smiled.

"Who knows? Perhaps I will go. If I do make

her laugh then, O my brothers, the laugh will be on you
for I shall become Tsar and you two will be known as
my two poor brothers. Ho! Ho! Ho! What a joke
that would be!"

Stefan laughed loud and heartily and his little sister
joined him, but his brothers looked at him sourly.

"He grows more foolish all the time!" they told
each other.

When they were gone to bed, Militza slipped over
to Stefan and whispered in his ear:

"Brother, you must go to the Princess. Tell her the
story that begins: *In my young days when I was an old,
old man. . . .* I think she'll just have to laugh, and
if she laughs then she can eat and she must be very
hungry by this time."

At first Stefan said no, he wouldn't go, but Militza
insisted and finally, to please her, he said he would.

So early the next morning he dressed himself in his
fine Sunday shirt with its blue and red embroidery. He
put on his bright red Sunday sash and his long shiny
boots. Then he mounted his horse and before his brothers were awake rode off to the Tsar's castle.

There he awaited his turn to be admitted to the Princess's chamber. When he came in he was so young
and healthy and vigorous that he seemed to bring with

him a little of the freshness of outdoors. The first lady-
in-waiting looked at him askance for without doubt he
was a farmer lad and his table manners probably were
not good. Well, he was a farmer lad and for that reason he didn't know that she was first lady-in-waiting.
He glanced at her once and thought: "What an ugly
old woman!" and thereafter he didn't think of her at
all. He glanced likewise at the Tsar and the Tsar
reminded him of a bull of his own. He wasn't afraid
of the bull, so why be afraid of the Tsar?

Suddenly he saw the Princess lying in bed with her
lovely hair spread out on the pillow like a golden fan
and for a moment he couldn't speak. Then he knelt
beside the bed and kissed her hand.

"Princess," he said, "I'm not learned and I'm not
clever and I don't suppose I can succeed where so many
wise men have failed. And even if I do make you
laugh you won't have to marry me unless you want to
because the reason I really came was to please Militza."

"Militza?"

"Yes, Princess, my little sister, Militza. She loves
me very much and so she thinks the stories I tell are
funny and she laughs at them. Last night she said to
me: 'Stefan, you must go to the Princess and tell her
the story that begins: *In my young days when I was an*

old, old man. . . . I think she'll just have to laugh and if she laughs then she can eat and she must be very hungry by this time.'"

"I am," the Princess said, with a catch in her voice. Then she added: "I think I like that little sister of yours and I think I like you, too. I wish you would tell me the story that begins: *In my young days when I was an old, old man.* . . ."

"But, Princess, it's a very foolish story."

"The foolisher, the better!"

Just here the first lady-in-waiting tried to correct the Princess for of course she should have said: "The more foolish, the better!" but the Tsar shut her up with a black frown and one fierce, "Wow!"

"Well, then," Stefan began:

In my young days when I was an old, old man I used to count my bees every morning. It was easy enough to count the bees but not the beehives because I had too many hives. One day when I finished counting I found that my best bee was missing. At once I saddled a rooster and set out to find him.

"Father!" cried the Princess. "Did you hear what Stefan said? He said he saddled his rooster!"

"Umph!" muttered the Tsar, and the first lady-in-waiting said severely:

"Princess, do not interrupt! Young man, continue."

His track led to the sea which I rode across on a bridge. The first thing I saw on the other side of the sea was my bee. There he was in a field of millet harnessed to a plow. "That's my bee!" I shouted to the man who was driving him. "Is that so?" the man said, and without any words he gave me back my bee and handed me a bag of millet to pay for the plowing. I took the bag and tied it securely on the bee. Then I unsaddled the rooster and mounted the bee. The rooster, poor thing, was so tired that I had to take him by the hand and lead him along beside us.

"Father!" the Princess cried, "did you hear that? He took the rooster by the hand! Isn't that funny!"

"Umph!" grunted the Tsar, and the first lady-in-waiting whispered:

"Hush! Let the young man finish!"

Whilst we were crossing the bridge, the string of the bag broke and all my millet spilled out. When night came I tied the rooster to the bee and lay down on the

*seashore to sleep. During the night some wolves came
and killed my bee and when I woke up I found that all
the honey had run out of his body. There was so much
honey that it rose up and up until it reached the ankles
of the valleys and the knees of the mountains. I took a
hatchet and swam down to a forest where I found two
deer leaping about on one leg. I shot at the deer with
my hatchet, killed them, and skinned them. With the
skins I made two leather bottles. I filled these with the
honey and strapped them over the rooster's back. Then
I rode home. I no sooner arrived home than my father
was born. " We must have holy water for the christen-
ing," I said. " I suppose I must go to heaven to fetch
some." But how was I to get there? I thought of my
millet. Sure enough the dampness had made it grow so
well that its tops now reached the sky. So all I had to do
was to climb a millet stalk and there I was in heaven.
Up there they had mown down some of my millet which
they baked into a loaf and were eating with boiled milk.
" That's my millet!" I said. " What do you want for
it? " they asked me. " I want some holy water to chris-
ten my father who has just been born." So they gave
me some holy water and I prepared to descend again to
earth. But on earth there was a violent storm going on
and the wind carried away my millet. So there I was*

with no way of getting down. I thought of my hair. It was so long that when I stood up it covered my ears and when I lay down it reached all the way to earth. So I pulled out a hair, tied it to a tree of heaven, and began descending by it. When it grew dark I made a knot in the hair and just sat where I was. It was cold, so I took a needle which I happened to have in my coat, split it up, and lighted a fire with the chips.

"Oh, father!" the Princess cried, "Stefan says he split a needle into kindling wood! Isn't he funny!"

"If you ask me—" the first lady-in-waiting began, but before she could say more the Tsar reached over and stepped on her toe so hard that she was forced to end her sentence with a little squeally, "Ouch!" The Princess, you see, was smiling and the Tsar was hoping that presently she would burst into a laugh. So he motioned Stefan to continue.

Then I lay down beside the fire and fell asleep. While I slept a spark from the fire fell on the hair and burned it through. I fell to earth with such force that I sank into the ground up to my chest. I couldn't budge, so I was forced to go home and get a spade and dig myself out. On the way home I crossed a field

Stefan Tells the Princess a Story

*where the reapers were cutting corn. The heat was so
great that they had to stop work. " I'll get our mare," I
said, " and then you'll feel cooler." You know our
mare is two days long and as broad as midnight and
she has willow trees growing on her back. So I ran and
got her and she cast such a cool shadow that the reapers
were. at once able to go back to work. Now they wanted
some fresh drinking water, but when they went to the
river they found it had frozen over.. They came back
to me and asked me would I get them some water.
" Certainly," I said. I went to the river myself, then
I took off my head and with it I broke a hole in the
ice. After that it was easy enough to fetch them some
water. " But where is your head?" they asked. " Oh!"
I said, " I must have forgotten it!"*

" Oh, father!" the Princess cried with a loud laugh,
" he says he forgot his head! Then, Stefan, what did
you do? What did you do?"

*I ran back to the river and got there just as a fox
was sniffing at my skull. " Hi, there!" I said, pulling
the fox's tail. The fox turned around and gave me a
paper on which was written these words: NOW THE
PRINCESS CAN EAT FOR SHE HAS*

LAUGHED AND STEFAN AND HIS LIT-
TLE SISTER ARE VERY HAPPY.

"What nonsense!" the first lady-in-waiting murmured with a toss of her head.

"Yes, beautiful nonsense!" the Princess cried, clap-
ping her hands and going off into peal after peal of
merry laughter. "Isn't it beautiful nonsense, father?
And isn't Stefan a dear lad? And, father, I'm awfully
hungry! Please have some food sent in at once and
Stefan must stay and eat with me."

So the Tsar had great trays of food brought in:
roast birds and vegetables and wheaten bread and many
kinds of little cakes and honey and milk and fruit.
And Stefan and the Princess ate and made merry and
the Tsar joined them and even the first lady-in-waiting
took one little cake which she crumbled in her handkerchief in a most refined manner.

Then Stefan rose to go and the Tsar said to him:

"Stefan, I will reward you richly. You have made
the Princess laugh and besides you have not insisted
on her marrying you. You are a fine lad and I shall
never forget you."

"But, father," the Princess said, "I don't want
Stefan to go. He amuses me and I like him. He said

I needn't marry him unless I wanted to but, father, I think I want to."

"Wow! Wow!" the Tsar roared. "What! My daughter marry the son of a farmer!"

"Now, father," the Princess said, "it's no use your *wow-wowing* at me and you know it isn't. If I can't marry Stefan I won't marry any one. And if I don't marry any one I'm going to stop eating again. So that's that!" And still holding Stefan's hand, the Princess turned her face to the wall.

What could the poor Tsar do? At first he fumed and raged but as usual after a day or two he came around to the Princess's way of thinking. In fact it soon seemed to him that Stefan had been his choice from the first and when one of his councilors remarked: "Then, Your Majesty, there's no use sending word to the neighboring kings that the Princess has reached a marriageable age and would like to look over their sons," the Tsar flew into an awful temper and roared:

"Wow! Wow! You blockhead! Neighboring kings, indeed, and their good-for-nothing sons! No, siree! The husband I want for my daughter is an honest farmer lad who knows how to work and how to play! That's the kind of son-in-law we need in this kingdom!"

So Stefan and the little Princess were married and
from that day the castle was no longer gloomy but
rang with laughter and merriment. Presently the people of the kingdom, following the example of their
rulers, were laughing, too, and cracking jokes and,
strange to say, they soon found they were working all
the better for their jollity.

Laughter grew so fashionable that even Mihailo and
Jakov were forced to take it up. They didn't do it
very well but they practised at it conscientiously.
Whenever people talked about Stefan, they always
pushed forward importantly and said:

"Ho! Ho! Ho! Do you mean Stefan, the Laughing Prince? Ha! Ha! Ha! Why, do you know,
he's our own brother!"

As for Militza, the Princess had her come to the
castle and said to her:

"I owe all my happiness to you, my dear, for you
it was who knew that of course I would laugh at
Stefan's nonsense! What sensible girl wouldn't?"

BEAUTY AND THE HORNS

The Story of an Enchanted Maiden

BEAUTY AND THE HORNS

THERE was once a rich man who when he was
dying called his son to his bedside and said:
"Danilo, my son, I am leaving you my riches. The
only thing I ask of you is this: close your ears to all
reports of an enchanted maiden who is known as Peerless Beauty and when the time comes that you wish
to marry choose for wife some quiet sensible girl of
your native village."

Now if the father had not mentioned Peerless Beauty
all might have been well. Danilo might never have
heard of her and after a time he would probably have
fallen in love with a girl of his native village and married her. As it was, after his father's death he kept
saying to himself:

"Peerless Beauty, the enchanted maiden of whom
my father warned me! I wonder is she really as beautiful as all that! I wonder where she lives!"

He thought about her until he could think of nothing else.

"Peerless Beauty! Peerless Beauty! Oh, I must
see this enchanted maiden even if it costs me my life!"

His father had a brother, a wise old man, who was supposed to know everything in the world.

"I will go to my uncle," the young man said. "Perhaps he will tell me where I can find Peerless Beauty."

So he went to his uncle and said:

"My dear uncle, my father as he lay dying told me about a wonderful maiden called Peerless Beauty. Can you tell me where she lives because I want to see her for myself and judge whether she is as beautiful as my father said."

His uncle looked at him gravely and shook his head.

"My poor boy, how can I tell you where that enchanted maiden lives when I know it would mean death to you if ever you saw her? Think no more about her but go, find some suitable maid in the village, and marry her like a sensible young man."

But his uncle's words, far from dissuading Danilo, only excited him the more.

"If my uncle knows where Peerless Beauty lives," he thought, "other men also know."

So one by one he went to all the old men in the village and asked them what they knew of Peerless Beauty. One by one they shook their heads and told him that Peerless Beauty was no maiden for him to be thinking about.

"Put her out of your mind," they said. "These enchanted maidens are a snare to young men. What you want to do is marry some quiet industrious girl here in the village and settle down like a sensible young man."

But the oftener Danilo heard this advice, the more firmly convinced he became that it was just what he did not want to do.

"Time enough to settle down after I've seen Peerless Beauty," he told himself. "She must be beautiful indeed, or all these old men would not be so anxious to keep me from seeing her. Well, if they won't tell me where she is, I'll go out in the world and find her for myself."

So he put on rich clothes as befitted his wealth, took a bag of the gold his father had left him, mounted his horse, and rode off into the world. Everywhere he went he made inquiries about Peerless Beauty and everywhere he found old men who knew about the enchanted maiden but would tell him nothing. Every one of them advised him to go home like a sensible young man and think no more about her. But all they said only made him the more determined to see the maiden for himself.

Finally one day as evening approached he came to

a little hut in the woods. At the door of the hut sat
a poor old woman. She held out her hand as he passed
and begged an alms. Danilo, being a kind hearted
young man, gave her a gold piece.

"May God reward you!" the old woman said.

"Granny," Danilo asked, "can you tell me the way
to Peerless Beauty?"

"Aye, my son, that I can but he is a rash youth
who seeks that maiden! It were better for you to turn
back than to go on!"

"But I'm not going to turn back!" Danilo declared.
"Whatever the outcome I'm going to find Peerless
Beauty and see for myself why all men fear her."

When the old woman saw that Danilo was determined, she gave up pleading with him and pointed out
a faint trail in the forest which, she told him, would
lead him to Peerless Beauty's castle.

He slept that night in the old woman's hut and
early next morning set out on the forest trail. By
afternoon he reached the castle.

"What do you want?" the guards demanded
roughly.

"I want to see Peerless Beauty."

"Have you gold?" they asked him.

Danilo showed them his bag of ducats.

They led him into a hall of the castle and told him to put his gold on a table. If he did so, perhaps Peerless Beauty would show herself and perhaps she wouldn't.

Danilo did as the guards directed and then faced a curtain behind which, they told him, Peerless Beauty was seated. The curtain opened a little, but instead of showing her face Peerless Beauty extended only one finger. However, that finger was so ravishingly beautiful that Danilo almost fainted with delight. He would have stayed gazing on that one enchanting finger for hours if the guards had not taken him roughly by the shoulders and thrown him out of the castle.

"Come again when you've got more gold!" they shouted after him.

Like a man in a dream Danilo rode back to the old woman's hut.

"Now, my son, are you satisfied?" she asked him. "Are you ready now to go home and settle down like a sensible young man?"

"Oh, granny!" Danilo raved. "Such a finger! I must see that finger again if it cost me my whole fortune!"

He slept that night in the old woman's hut and the next day returned to his native village. There he got another bag of the golden ducats which his father had left him and at once started back to the castle of Peerless Beauty.

This time that heartless maiden stripped him again of his gold, showed him two of her enchanting fingers, and as before had her guards throw him out of the castle.

" Come again when you've got more gold! " they shouted after him.

That's exactly what the poor young man did. He went back and back until the fortune that his father had left him was entirely squandered. And all he had seen of Peerless Beauty up to that time were the fingers of one hand! Shouldn't you suppose that now with all his wealth lost he would get over his foolish infatuation? Well, he didn't.

" I must go back again! " he kept telling himself.

His gold was gone but he still had his father's house. It was a big old house with garrets and cellars.

" Perhaps if I hunt I shall find some treasures hidden away in odd corners," Danilo said.

So he hunted upstairs and down. He opened old boxes and rummaged about among the dark rafters. One day he came upon a funny looking little cap.

" I wonder whose this was," he thought to himself.

He went to a mirror and tried the cap on. Then a strange thing happened. The moment the cap touched his head, Danilo disappeared.

"Ah!" he cried, "it's a magic cap and the moment I put it on I become invisible! Now I can slip into Peerless Beauty's chamber and see her lovely face!"

With his magic cap pulled tightly down over his forehead, he set off once more for Peerless Beauty's castle. Sure enough he was able to pass unseen the guards at the gate, he was able to go boldly into the great hall, and beyond it through the curtain into Peerless Beauty's own chamber.

The Beauty was seated with her back to the curtain and a serving maid was combing out her hair for the night. It was lovely hair and it fell down over Beauty's shoulders like a mantle of gold. At mere sight of it Danilo was so overcome with emotion that he sighed.

"What's that?" Beauty cried. "There's some one in my chamber!"

The serving maid looked under the bed and behind the chairs and in the corners.

"There's no one here, my lady."

"That's strange!" Beauty said. "I feel as though some one were looking at me."

When Danilo saw the actual face of the enchanted maiden, it was all he could do to keep from crying aloud. She was so unutterably beautiful that he almost swooned away in ecstacy.

Presently the maiden went to bed and fell into an uneasy sleep. The light of a single candle shed a faint radiance over her face making it lovelier than ever. Through all the long hours of night Danilo stood perfectly still, gazing at her, afraid almost to breathe lest he should disturb her.

"Unless I win her for wife," he thought to himself, "I shall nevermore be happy!"

When morning came the maiden awoke with a start and said:

"There's some one looking at me! Who is it? Who is it?"

"It's only your poor Danilo," a voice answered.

"Danilo? Who is Danilo?"

"The youth whom you have been treating so cruelly. But though you have treated me cruelly, I love you still!"

"If you love me still," the maiden said, "let me see you."

Danilo took off the magic cap and there he stood, a handsome youth, at the foot of her bed. Then the crafty maiden spoke him fair and Danilo told her about the magic cap, and when she said to him that she repented having treated him so cruelly and asked him to let her see the cap, the poor young man was so dazzled by her beauty and her seeming kindness that he handed it to her at once.

Instantly she clapped it on her head and disappeared. Then she laughed in derision and called out loudly to the guards:

"Ho, there! Take out this young man and drive him forth! Let him return when he has another treasure to offer me!"

So the guards dragged Danilo out and drove him away.

With no more gold, with no more magic cap, Danilo returned to his father's house.

"Perhaps there are other treasures hidden away," he thought. "I'll search further."

In his search he came upon an old pitcher and thinking it might be silver he began rubbing it. Instantly there was a clap of thunder and a company of soldiers appeared. Their captain saluted Danilo respectfully and said:

"We are the servants of that magic pitcher. What does our master wish?"

" Magic pitcher? " stammered Danilo. " And am I your master? "

" Yes," said the captain, " you are our master as long as you hold the magic pitcher in your hands."

" You may disappear now," Danilo said. " I will rub the pitcher when I need you."

Delighted with this unexpected good fortune, he hurried off to the woods to the hut of the old woman who had befriended him before. He showed her the pitcher and demonstrated for her how it worked. Then he asked her to carry a message to Peerless Beauty.

" Tell her," he said, " that unless she consents to marry me at once I'll lead a mighty army against her, take her captive, and then send her off in exile to that howling wilderness which people call the Donkeys' Paradise."

" I will deliver your message," the old woman said, " on condition that you promise me to be on your guard this time. Don't let the maiden trick you again. She is under an enchantment that makes her cruel and crafty and the enchantment will never be broken until she meets a man upon whom her wiles have no effect."

" Trust me this time," Danilo said. " I've had my lesson."

So the old woman delivered the message and when

Peerless Beauty received it with scorn, Danilo at once
set out for the castle with the magic pitcher in his hand.
He began rubbing and every time he rubbed a company
of soldiers appeared.   Soon the castle was surrounded
by a great army and in fright and dismay Peerless
Beauty sent out word that she was ready to make an
unconditional surrender.

When Danilo entered the castle he found her humble
and meek.

" I have treated you cruelly," she said. " Now I am
in your power, do with me what you will."   And she
began weeping softly until the sight of her tears drove
Danilo distracted.

" Weep no more, dear lady! " he cried. " You have
nothing to fear from me! I love you! I am your
slave! "

The Peerless one slowly dried her tears.

" If you love me as you say you do, you will tell me
by what magic you have raised this great army."

Then Danilo, forgetting the old woman's warning,
took the magic pitcher out of his shirt and showed the
maiden how it worked.

" Ah! " she murmured wonderingly. " It looks like
any old pitcher! Please, Danilo, let me see it in my
own hands."

Danilo handed her the pitcher and, quick as a flash, she rubbed it. There was a clap of thunder, a company of soldiers appeared, and their captain saluting her respectfully said:

"What does the mistress of the pitcher want?"

"Nay!" cried Danilo, "it is I who own the pitcher, not she!"

"We are the servants," the captain said, "of whoever holds the pitcher."

At that Peerless Beauty laughed loud and scornfully until the castle rang with her merriment.

"Seize that wretch!" she said, pointing to Danilo. "Tie his hands and drive him out in exile to the Donkeys' Paradise! Let him stay there until he has another treasure to present me!"

So they drove Danilo out to the wilderness and left him there.

He wandered about for many days hungry and thirsty, subsisting on roots and berries, and having for drink only the water that collected in the hoof prints of the wild beasts.

"See what I've come to!" he cried aloud. "Why didn't I heed the old woman's warning! If I had, I should have broken the evil enchantment that binds my Peerless Beauty and all would have been well!"

One day as he wandered about he came upon a vine that was laden with great clusters of luscious red grapes. He fell upon them ravenously and ate bunch after bunch. Suddenly he felt something in his hair and lifting his hands he found that horns had grown out all over his head.

" Fine grapes these are! " he exclaimed, " to bring out horns on a person's head! "

However, he was so hungry that he kept on eating until his head was one mass of horns.

The next day he found a vine that had clusters of white grapes. He began eating the white grapes and he hadn't finished a bunch before the horns all fell off his head.

" Ha! " he said. " The red grapes put horns on and the white grapes take them off! That's a trick worth knowing! "

He took some reeds and fashioned two baskets one of which he filled with red grapes and the other with white grapes. Then staining his face with the dark juice of a leaf until he looked brown and sunburned like a countryman, he went back to Peerless Beauty's castle. There he marched up and down below the Peerless one's window crying his wares like a huckster:

"Sweet grapes for sale! Who wants my fresh sweet grapes!"

Now it was not the season for grapes, so Peerless Beauty when she heard the cry was surprised and said to her serving maid:

"Go quickly and buy me some grapes from that huckster and mind you don't eat one yourself!"

The serving maid hurried out to Danilo and he sold her some of the red grapes. As she carried them in, she couldn't resist the temptation of slipping a few into her mouth. Instantly some horns grew out on her head.

"That's to punish me for disobeying my mistress!" the poor girl cried. "Oh, dear, what shall I do?"

She was afraid to show herself to Peerless Beauty, so she pretended she was taken sick and she went to bed and pulled the sheet over her head and sent in the grapes by another serving maid.

Peerless Beauty ate them all before she discovered their frightful property. Then there was a great to-do, and cries of anger and of fright, and a quick sending out of the guards to find the huckster. But the huckster had disappeared.

What could Peerless Beauty do now? She tried to

pull the horns out but they wouldn't come. She tried
to cut them off but they resisted the edge of the sharp-
est knife. She was too proud to show herself with
horns, so she swathed her head with jewels and ribbons and pretended she was wearing an elaborate head-
dress.

Then she sent heralds through the land offering a
huge reward to any one who could cure her serving
maid of some strange horns that had grown out on her
head. You see she thought if she could get hold of
some one who would cure the maid, then she could
make him cure her, too.

Well, doctors and quacks and all sorts of people
came and tried every kind of remedy, but all in vain.
The horns stayed firmly rooted.

A whole week went by and when the last of the
quacks had come and gone, Danilo, disguised as an old
physician, presented himself and craved audience with
the Peerless one. He carried two small jars in his
hands one of which was filled with a conserve made
from the white grapes and the other with a conserve
made from the red grapes.

Peerless Beauty, her horns swathed in silk and gleaming with jewels, received him coldly.

" Are you one more quack? " she asked.

"Not a quack," he said, bowing low, "but a man who has happened upon a strange secret of nature. I can cure your serving maid of her horns provided she confess to me all her misdeeds and hand over to me anything she has that does not belong to her."

Peerless Beauty had him shown to the room where the serving maid lay in bed. The poor frightened girl at once confessed that she had stolen a few of her mistress's grapes and eaten them. Danilo spoke kindly to her, gave her some of the white grape conserve, and as soon as she had tasted it the horns of course dropped off.

Thereupon Peerless Beauty led Danilo to her own chamber, ordered all her people out, and then acknowledged that she, too, was suffering from horns.

"I am sure I can cure you," Danilo told her, "provided you confess to me all your misdeeds and hand over to me whatever you have that belongs to some one else."

"I cheated a foolish young man out of five bags of gold," Peerless Beauty said. "Here they are in this chest. Take them."

Danilo opened the chest and took out his own five bags of gold.

"Is that all?" he asked.

The Magic Pitcher

" Yes, that is all."

Danilo gave her some of the red grape conserve and of course, instead of the horns already on her head falling off, more grew on.

" You're not telling me the truth," Danilo said, " and I can't cure you. There's no use my treating you further."

He turned to go and Peerless Beauty, in great fright, begged him to stay.

" I do remember another misdeed," she confessed. " I took by trickery a magic pitcher from the same foolish young man."

She gave Danilo the pitcher and he hid it in his shirt.

" Is that all? "

" Yes, that is all."

Danilo gave her some more of the red grape conserve and, of course, more horns grew out on her head. Then he pretended to get angry.

" How can you expect to be cured when you don't tell me the truth? I told you I could not cure you unless you confessed all! "

Peerless Beauty wanted much to keep the magic cap but when the strange physician thundered and scowled and threatened again to leave her, more horned than ever, she acknowledged that she had taken the cap, too, and handed it over.

This time Danilo gave her some of the white grape conserve and as soon as she had eaten it all the horns fell off and her head shimmered and shone as of old with her beautiful hair.

Then Danilo told her who he was and at once the maiden sought to ensnare him again with her wiles.

" What a wonderful man you are, Danilo! I could love you now if you loved me, but I know of course that you will never love me again after the cruel way I have treated you! "

" But I do love you! " Danilo cried. " I do love you! "

" No, you don't! " she said, and she pretended to weep. " If you did love me, you'd tell me where you found those red grapes and what this magic conserve is made of. But of course you don't love me enough to tell me."

Because she looked more beautiful than ever with the tears on her lovely cheeks, Danilo was about to tell her what she wanted to know when he remembered the old woman's warning. That was enough. He hardened his heart and declared:

"No! I'll never tell you! Do you hear me: I'll never tell you!"

She wept and implored him and used all her wiles, but Danilo remembering the past was firm. And presently he had the reward that a man always has when he's firm, for as soon as it was evident that she could no longer befool him, the evil enchantment that bound her broke with a snap and Peerless Beauty became a human maiden as gentle and sweet and loving as she was beautiful.

She knelt at Danilo's feet and humbly begged his pardon and promised, if he would still marry her, to make him the most dutiful wife in the world.

So Danilo married Peerless Beauty and with the servants of the magic pitcher transported her and her castle and her riches together with the old woman who had befriended them both to his own native village. There he still lives happy and prosperous.

His uncle and all the old men in the village take credit to themselves for the success of his adventures.

"It is due entirely to us," they tell any one who will listen to them, "that Danilo went out in search of Peerless Beauty in the first place. When he came to us and asked our advice we said to him: 'Go, by all means! You're young and brave and of course you'll win her!' If we hadn't urged him to go, he would probably have settled down here at home, married some quiet village girl, and never be heard of again!"

That's how the old men talk now, but we know what they really did say at the time!

Yet after all that doesn't matter. All that matters is that Danilo and Peerless Beauty love each other and are happy.

THE PIGEON'S BRIDE

The Story of a Princess Who Kissed and Told

THE PIGEON'S BRIDE

THERE was once a King who had an only daughter. She was as lovely as a princess ought to be and by the time she reached a marriageable age the fame of her beauty had spread far and wide over all the world. Neighboring kings and even distant ones were already sending envoys to her father's court begging permission to offer their sons as suitors to the Princess's hand. As he had no son of his own the Princess's father was delighted that the day was fast approaching when he might have a son-in-law, and long before even the name of any particular prince was discussed the Princess's mother had planned the wedding down to its last detail.

The Princess alone was uninterested.

"I'm not ready to get married yet," she'd say to her parents every day when they'd begin telling her about the various princes who were anxious to gain her favor. "Why such haste? I'm young and there's plenty of time. Besides, just now I'm too busy with my embroidery to be bothered with a crowd of young men."

With that, before the King could reprove her, the

Princess would throw her arms about his neck, kiss him under the corner of his mustache, and go flying off to the tower-room where she had her embroidery frame.

Her mother, the Queen, was much upset by the Princess's attitude.

" In my youth," she said, " girls were not like this. We were brought up to think that courtship and marriage were the most important events in our lives. I don't know what's getting into the heads of the young girls nowadays! "

But the King, who was still smiling from the tickling little kiss which the Princess had planted under the corner of his mustache, always answered:

" Tut! Tut! We needn't worry yet! Take my word for it when some particular young man comes along she'll be interested fast enough! "

At this the Queen, ending the discussion every day with the same words, would shake her head and declare:

" I tell you it isn't natural for a girl to be more interested in embroidery than in a long line of handsome young suitors! "

The Princess was interested in her embroidery— there's no doubt about that. She spent every moment she could in the tower-room, working and singing. The tower was high up among the treetops. It was reached by winding stairs so narrow and so many that no one any older than the Princess would care to climb them. The Princess flew up them like a bird, scarcely pausing for breath. At the top of the stairs was a trap-door which was the only means of entrance into the tower-room. Once in the tower-room with the bolt of the trap-door securely fastened, the Princess was safe from interruption and could work away at her embroidery to her heart's content. The tower had windows on all sides, so the Princess as she sat at her embroidery frame could look out north, east, south, and west.

The clouds sailed by in the sky, the wind blew and at once the leaves in the treetops began murmuring and whispering among themselves, and the birds that went flying all over the world would often alight on some branch near the tower and sing to the Princess as she worked or chatter some exciting story that she could almost understand.

"What!" the Princess would think to herself as she looked out north, east, south, and west. "Leave my tower and my beautiful embroidery to become the wife of some conceited young man! Never!"

From this remark you can understand perfectly well that the particular young man of whom her father spoke had not yet come along. And I'm sure you'll also know that shutting herself up in the tower-room and bolting the trap-door was not going to keep him away when it was time for him to come. Yet I don't believe that you'd have recognized him when he did come any more than the Princess did. This is how it happened:

One afternoon when as usual she was working at her embroidery and singing as she worked, suddenly there was a flutter of wings at the eastern window and a lovely Pigeon came flying into the room. It circled three times about the Princess's head and then alighted on the embroidery frame. The Princess reached out her hand and the bird, instead of taking fright, allowed her to stroke its gleaming neck. Then she took it gently in her hands and fondled it to her bosom, kissing its bill and smoothing its plumage with her lips.

"You beautiful thing!" she cried. "How I love you!"

"If you really love me," the Pigeon said, "have a bowl of milk here at this same hour to-morrow and then we'll see what we'll see."

With that the bird spread its wings and flew out the western window.

The Princess was so excited that for the rest of the afternoon she forgot her embroidery.

" Did the Pigeon really speak? " she asked herself as she stood staring out the western window, " or have I been dreaming? "

The next day when she climbed the winding stairs she went slowly for she carried in her hands a brimming bowl of milk.

" Of course it won't come again! " she said, and she made herself sit down quietly before the embroidery frame and work just as though she expected nothing.

But exactly at the same hour as the day before there was a flutter of wings at the eastern window, the sound of a gentle *coo! coo!* and there was the Pigeon ready to be loved and caressed.

" You beautiful creature! " the Princess cried, kissing its coral beak and smoothing its neck with her lips, " how I love you! And see, I have brought you the bowl of milk that you asked for! "

The bird flew over to the bowl, poised for a moment on its brim, then splashed into the milk as though to take a bath.

The Princess laughed and clapped her hands and then, as she looked, she saw a strange thing happen. The bird's feathers opened like a shirt and out of the feather shirt stepped a handsome youth.

(You remember I told you how surprised the Princess was going to be. And you're surprised, too, aren't you?)

He was so handsome that all the Princess could say was, "Oh!"

He came slowly towards her and knelt before her.

"Dear Princess," he said, "do not be frightened. If it had not been for your sweet words yesterday when you said you loved me I should never have been able to leave this feather shirt. Do not turn from me now because I am a man and not a pigeon. Love me still if you can, for I love you. It was because I fell in love with you yesterday when I saw you working at your embroidery that I flew in by the open window and let you caress me."

For a long time the Princess could only stare at the kneeling youth, too amazed to speak. He was so handsome that she forgot all about the pigeon he used to be, she forgot her embroidery, she forgot everything. She hadn't supposed that any young man in the whole world could be so handsome! Why, just looking at him, she could be happy forever and ever and ever!

"Would you rather I were still a pigeon?" the young man asked.

"No! No! No!" the Princess cried. "I like you ever so much better this way!"

The young man gravely bowed his head and kissed her hand and the Princess blushed and trembled and wished he would do it again. She had never imagined that any kiss could be so wonderful!

They passed the afternoon together and it seemed to the Princess it was the happiest afternoon of all her life. As the sun was sinking the youth said:

"Now I must leave you and become a pigeon again."

"But you'll come back, won't you?" the Princess begged.

"Yes, I'll come back to-morrow but on one condition: that you don't tell any one about me. I'll come back every day at the same hour but if ever you tell about me then I won't be able to come back any more."

"I'll never tell!" the Princess promised.

Then the youth kissed her tenderly, dipped himself in the milk, went back into his feather shirt, and flew off as a pigeon.

The next day he came again and the next and the next and the Princess fell so madly in love with him that all day long and all night long, too, she thought of nothing else. She no longer touched her embroidery but day after day sat idle in the tower-room just awaiting the hour of his arrival. And every day it seemed to the King and the Queen and all the people about

the Court that the Princess was becoming more and
more beautiful. Her cheeks kept growing pinker, her
eyes brighter, her lovely hair more golden.

"I must say sitting at that foolish embroidery agrees
with her," the King said.

"No, it isn't that," the Queen told him. "It's the
big bowl of milk she drinks every afternoon. You
know milk is very good for the complexion."

"Milk indeed!" murmured the Princess to herself,
and she blushed rosier than ever at thought of her wonderful secret.

But a princess can't keep growing more and more
beautiful without everybody in the world hearing about
it. The neighboring kings soon began to feel angry
and suspicious.

"What ails this Princess?" they asked among themselves. "Isn't one of our sons good enough for her?
Is she waiting for the King of Persia to come as a suitor
or what? Let us stand together on our rights and
demand to know why she won't consider one of our
sons!"

So they sent envoys to the Princess's father and
he saw at once that the matter had become serious.

"My dear," he said to the Princess, "your mother
and I have humored you long enough. It is high time

that you had a husband and I insist that you allow the sons of neighboring kings to be presented to you next week."

" I won't do it! " the Princess declared. " I'm not interested in the sons of the neighboring kings and that's all there is about it! "

Her father looked at her severely.

" Is that the way for a princess to talk? Persist in this foolishness and you may embroil your country in war! "

" I don't care! " the Princess cried, bursting into tears. " I can't marry any of them, so why let them be presented? "

" Why can't you marry any of them? "

" I just can't! " the Princess insisted.

At first, in spite of the pleadings of both parents, she would tell them no more, but her mother kept questioning her until at last in self-defense the Princess confessed that she had a true love who came to her in the tower every afternoon in the form of a pigeon.

" He's a prince," she told them, " the son of a distant king. At present he is under an enchantment that turns him into a pigeon. When the enchantment is broken he is coming as a prince to marry me."

" My poor child! " the Queen cried. " Think no more

about this Pigeon Prince! The enchantment may last
a hundred years and then where will you be!"

"But he is my love!" the Princess declared, "and if
I can't have him I won't have any one!"

When the King found that nothing they could say
would move her from this resolution, he sighed and murmured:

"Very well, my dear. If it must be so, it must be.
This afternoon when your lover comes, bring him down
to me that I may talk to him."

But that afternoon the Pigeon did not come. Nor
the next afternoon either, nor the next, and then too
late the Princess remembered his warning that if she
told about him he could never come back.

So now she sat in the tower-room idle and heartbroken, reproaching herself that she had betrayed her
lover and praying God to forgive her and send him back
to her. And the roses faded from her cheeks and her
eyes grew dull and the people about the Court began
wondering why they had ever thought her the most
beautiful princess in the world.

At last she went to the King, her father, and said:

"As my love can no longer come back to me because
I forgot my promise and betrayed him, I must go out
into the world and hunt him. Unless I find him life

will not be worth the living. So do not oppose me, father, but help me. Have three pairs of iron shoes made for me and three iron staffs. I will wander over the wide world until these are worn out and then, if by that time I have not found him, I will come home to you."

So the King had three pairs of iron shoes made for the Princess and three iron staffs and she set forth on her quest. She traveled through towns and cities and many kingdoms, over rough mountains and desert places, looking everywhere for her enchanted love. But nowhere could she find any trace of him.

At the end of the first year she had worn out the first pair of iron shoes and the first iron staff. At the end of the second year she had worn out the second pair of iron shoes and the second iron staff. At the end of the third year, when she had worn out the third pair of iron shoes and the third staff, she returned to her father's palace looking thin and worn and sad.

"My poor child," the King said, "I hope now you realize that the Pigeon Prince is gone forever. Think no more about him. Go back to your embroidery and when the roses begin blooming in your cheeks again we'll find some young prince for you who isn't enchanted."

But the Princess shook her head.

"Let me try one thing more, father," she begged, "and then if I don't find my love I'll do as you say."

The King agreed to this.

"Well, then," the Princess said, "build a public bath-house and have the heralds proclaim that the King's daughter will sit at the entrance and will allow any one to bathe free of charge who will tell her the story of the strangest thing he has ever heard or seen."

So the King built the bath-house and sent out his heralds far and wide. Men and women from all over the world came and bathed and told the Princess stories of this marvel and that, but never, alas, a word of an enchanted pigeon.

The days went by and the Princess grew more and more discouraged.

"Isn't it sad," the courtiers began whispering, "how the Princess has lost her looks! Do you suppose she ever was really beautiful or did we just imagine it?"

And the neighboring kings when they heard this remarked softly among themselves:

"It's just as well we didn't hurry one of our sons into a marriage with this young woman!"

Now there was a poor widow who lived near the bath-

The Princess Kissed Its Coral Beak

house. She had a daughter, a pretty young girl, who used to sit at the window and watch the Princess as people came and told her their stories.

" Mother," the girl said one day, " every one in the world goes to the bath-house and I want to go, too! "

" Nonsense! " the mother said. " What story could you tell the Princess? "

" But everybody else goes and I don't see why I can't! "

" Well, my dear," the mother promised, " you may just as soon as you see or hear something strange. Talk no more about it now but go, fetch me a pitcher of water from the town well."

The girl obediently took an empty pitcher and went to the town well. Just as she had filled the pitcher she heard some one say:

" Mercy me, I fear I'll be late! "

She turned around and what do you think she saw? A rooster in wooden shoes with a basket under his wing!

" I fear I'll be late! I fear I'll be late! " the rooster kept repeating as he hurried off making a funny little clatter with his wooden shoes.

" How strange! " the girl thought to herself. " A rooster with wooden shoes! I'm sure the Princess would

love to hear about him! I'll follow him and see what
he does."

He went to a garden where he filled his basket with
fresh vegetables—with onions and beans and garlic.
Then he hurried home to a little house. The girl slipped
in after him and hid behind the door.

"Thank goodness, I'm on time!" the rooster murmured.

He put a big bowl on the table and filled it with
milk.

"There!" he said. "Now I'm ready for them!"

Presently twelve beautiful pigeons came flying in by
the open door. Eleven of them dipped in the bowl of
milk, their feather shirts opened, and out they stepped
eleven handsome youths. But the Twelfth Pigeon
perched disconsolately on the windowsill and remained
a pigeon. The eleven laughed at him and said:

"Poor fellow, your bride betrayed you, didn't she?
So you have to remain shut up in your feather shirt
while we go off and have a jolly time!"

"Yes," the Twelfth Pigeon said, "she broke her
promise and now she goes wandering up and down the
world hunting for me. If she doesn't find me I shall
nevermore escape the feather shirt but shall have to fly
about forever as a pigeon. But I know she will find me

for she will never stop until she does. And when she finds me, then the enchantment will be broken forever and I can marry her!"

The eleven youths went laughing arm in arm out of the house and in a few moments the solitary Pigeon flew after them. Instantly the girl slipped out from behind the door and hurried home with her pitcher of water. Then she ran quickly across to the bath-house and all out of breath she cried to the Princess:

"O Princess, I have such a wonderful story to tell you all about a rooster with wooden shoes and twelve pigeons only eleven of them are not pigeons but handsome young men and the twelfth one has to stay in his feather shirt because—"

At mention of the enchanted pigeons, the Princess turned pale. She held up her hand and made the girl pause until she had her breath, then she questioned her until she knew the whole story.

"It must be my love!" the Princess thought to herself. "Thank God I have found him at last!"

The next day at the same hour she went with the girl to the town well and when the rooster clattered by in his wooden shoes they followed him home and slipping into the house they hid behind the door and waited. Presently twelve pigeons flew in. Eleven of them dipped in the milk and came out handsome young men. The Twelfth sat disconsolately on the window sill and remained a pigeon. The eleven laughed at him and twitted him with having had a bride that had betrayed him. Then the eleven went away laughing arm in arm. Before the Twelfth could fly after them, the Princess ran out from behind the door and cried:

"My dear one, I have found you at last!"

The Pigeon flew into her hands and she took him and kissed his coral beak and smoothed his gleaming plumage with her lips. Then she put him in the milk and the feather shirt opened and her own true love stepped out.

She led him at once to her father and when the King found him well trained in all the arts a prince should know he accepted him as his future son-in-law and presented him to the people.

So after all the Princess's mother was able to give her daughter the gorgeous wedding she had planned for years and years. Preparations were begun at once but the Queen insisted on making such vast quantities of little round cakes and candied fruits and sweetmeats of all kinds that it was three whole months before the wedding actually took place. By that time the roses were again blooming in the Princess's cheeks, her eyes were brighter than before, and her long shining hair was more golden than ever.

All the neighboring kings were invited to the wedding and when they saw the bride they shook their heads sadly and said among themselves:

" Lost her looks indeed! What did people mean by saying such a thing? Why, she's the most beautiful princess in the world! What a pity she didn't marry one of our sons! "

But when they met the Prince of her choice, they saw at once why the Princess had fallen in love with him.

" Any girl would! " they said.

It was a big wedding, as I told you before, and the only guest present who was not a king or a queen or a royal personage of some sort was the poor girl who saw the rooster with wooden shoes in the first place. The Queen, of course, had wanted only royalty but the Princess declared that the poor girl was her dear friend and would have to be invited. So the Queen, when she saw that the Princess was set on having her own way, had the poor girl come to the palace before the wedding and decked her out in rich clothes until people were sure that she was some strange princess whom the bride had met on her travels.

"My dear," whispered the Princess as they sat down beside each other at the wedding feast, "how beautiful you look!"

"But I'm not as beautiful as you!" the girl said.

The Princess laughed.

"Of course not! No one can be as beautiful as I am because I have the secret of beauty!"

"Dear Princess," the poor girl begged, "won't you tell me the secret of beauty?"

The Princess leaned over and whispered something in the poor girl's ear.

It was only one word:

"Happiness!"

THE LITTLE LAME FOX

*The Story of the Youngest Brother Who Found the Magic
Grape-Vine and Married the Golden Maiden*

THE LITTLE LAME FOX

THERE was once a wealthy farmer who had three sons. The oldest was a selfish overbearing fellow. The second was a weak chap who always did everything his brother suggested. The youngest whose name was Janko was not as bright and clever as his brothers but he was honest and, moreover, he had a good heart and in this world a good heart, you know, is more likely to bring its owner happiness than wicked brains.

"That booby!" the oldest brother would say whenever he saw Janko. And the second would snicker and repeat the ugly word, "Booby!"

The father was proud of his three sons and happy to see them grow up strong and healthy.

"They're good boys," he'd say to himself, "and I'm a fortunate father."

Now there was one very curious thing about this farmer that nobody understood. One of his eyes was always laughing and the other was always weeping.

"What's the matter with your father's eyes?" people used to ask the sons.

The sons didn't know any more than any one else.

One day they were in the garden discussing the matter among themselves.

"Why don't we just go and ask him?". Janko suggested.

"If anybody is to ask him, I will!" declared the oldest brother importantly.

So he went indoors to his father and said:

"Father, people are forever talking about your eyes. Now I wish you would tell me why one of them is always laughing and the other always weeping."

"My eyes, indeed!" cried the farmer, and in a rage he snatched up a knife and hurled it straight at his son. The young man dodged aside and fled and the knife stuck in the door jamb.

All out of breath the oldest brother returned to the others but of course he was ashamed to tell them what had happened. So he said to them:

"If you want to know what's the matter with father's eyes, you'll have to ask him yourselves."

So the second brother went in to the farmer and he had exactly the same experience. When he came out he gave his older brother a wink and said to Janko:

"Now it is your turn, Booby. Father is waiting for you."

So Janko went in to his father and said:

" You have told my brothers why one of your eyes is always laughing and the other always weeping. Now please tell me for I, too, want to know."

In a rage the farmer snatched up the knife again and lifted his arm to hurl it. But Janko stood perfectly still. Why should he turn and run away as though he had done something wrong? He had only asked his father a civil question and if his father did not wish to answer it, he could tell him so.

The farmer when he saw that the boy was not to be frightened smiled and laid the knife aside.

" Thank God," he said, " I have one son who is not a coward! I have been waiting these many years to have my sons ask me this very question. My right eye laughs because God has blessed me and made me rich and has allowed my three sons to grow to manhood, strong and healthy. My left eye weeps because I can never forget a Magic Grape-Vine which once grew in my garden. It used to give me a bucket of wine every hour of the twenty-four! One night a thief came and stole my Magic Vine and I have never heard of it since. Do you wonder that my left eye weeps at the memory of this wonderful Vine? Alas, the bucket of wine that used to flow out of it every hour of the day and night— I have never tasted its like since! "

"Father," Janko said, "dry your weeping eye! I and my brothers will go out into the world and find your Magic Grape-Vine wherever it is hidden!"

With that Janko ran out to his brothers and when they heard what he had to say they laughed and called him, "Booby!" and asked him didn't he suppose that they had already planned to do just this thing. Of course they hadn't, but they were so jealous and ill-natured that they couldn't bear the thought of his being the first to suggest anything.

"We mustn't lose any more time," Janko said.

"It doesn't matter how much time you lose, Mr. Booby! As for us we two are going to start out to-morrow at sunrise."

"But, brothers," Janko begged, "please let me go, too!"

"No!" they told him shortly. "You can stay home and look after the farm!"

But their father when he heard the discussion said, no, Janko was also to go as he was the bravest of them all. After that the brothers, because they didn't want their father to tell how they had been afraid and run away, had to agree.

So the next morning early the three of them started out, each with a wallet well-stocked with food.

"How are we going to get rid of the Booby?" the second one whispered.

"Trust me!" the oldest one whispered back with a wink.

Presently they came to a crossroads where three roads branched. Now the oldest brother knew that after a short distance two of the roads came together again. So he motioned the second brother slyly that he was to take the middle road. Then he said:

"Brothers, let us part here and each take a different road. Do you agree?"

"Yes," the other two said, "we agree."

"Then suppose Janko take the left-hand road."

"And I'll take the middle road," the second cried.

"And I," the eldest said, "will take the one that's left. So farewell, brothers, and let us meet here in a year's time."

"God bless us all," Janko called out, "and grant that one of us may find our dear father's Magic Grape-Vine."

The two older brothers of course met in a short time when their roads joined and they had a good laugh to think how they had outwitted the Booby.

"Time enough to look for that old Grape-Vine when we've had a little fun!" the eldest said. "Let us sit down here and eat a bite and then push on to the next village. There's an inn there where we can try our luck at cards."

So they sat down by the roadside, opened their wallets, and laid out some bread and cheese. Just then a Little Lame Fox came limping up on three feet, and whimpering and fawning it begged for something to eat.

"Get out!" bawled the older brother and the second, picking up a handful of stones, threw them at the Fox.

The little animal shied and then came timidly back, again begging for something to eat.

"Let's kill it!" cried one of the brothers.

They both jumped up and tried to strike the little creature with their sticks. The Fox limped off and they followed, hitting at it as they ran and always just missing it. It was so weak and lame that they expected every minute to overtake it and so kept on chasing it until it had led them pretty far into the woods. Then suddenly it disappeared and there was nothing left for the brothers to do but make their way back to the roadside grumbling and cursing. In their absence some shepherd dogs had found their open wallets and eaten all their food. So now they really had something to curse about.

Janko meanwhile had been trudging along steadily on the third road. At last when he began to feel hungry, he sat down by the wayside and opened his wallet. Instantly the same Little Lame Fox came limping up and whimpered and fawned and begged for something to eat.

"You poor little creature," Janko said, "are you hungry?"

He held out his hand coaxingly and the animal gave it a timid sniff.

"Of course I'll give you something to eat," Janko said. "There's enough for both of us."

With that he divided his bread and cheese and gave the Little Fox half. Then they ate together and the Little Fox allowed Janko to pat her head.

When they finished eating the Fox sat up on her haunches and said:

"Now, Janko, tell me about yourself. Who are you and where are you going?"

The Fox seemed such a sensible little person that it didn't surprise Janko in the least to have her sit up and talk. Janko's brothers would have said that he hadn't sense enough to be surprised. But he had a good heart, Janko had, and as you'll soon hear a good heart is a much better guide for conduct than wicked brains.

Janko answered the Fox simply and truthfully. He told about his father and his two brothers and about his father's weeping eye and the Magic Grape-Vine for which he and his brothers were gone in search.

"You've been good to me," the Little Fox said. "You've shared your bread with me and that makes us friends. So from now on if you'll be a brother to me, I'll be a little sister to you."

Goodness knows Janko's own brothers weren't very good to him, but Janko understood what the Little Fox meant and he agreed.

"Well then, brother," the Fox said, "I know where that Grape-Vine is and I'm going to help you to get it. If you do just as I say I don't believe you'll have any trouble. Now take hold of my tail and away we'll go."

So Janko took hold of the Little Fox's tail and sure enough away they went. Whether they sailed through the air or just ran fleetly along the ground I don't know. But I do know that they went a great distance and that when they stopped Janko didn't feel in the least tired or breathless.

"Now, my brother," the Little Fox said, "listen carefully to what I tell you. The king of this country has a wonderful garden. In the midst of it your father's Grape-Vine is planted. We are close to the garden now. It is protected by twelve watches each of which is composed of twelve guards. To get to the Grape-Vine you will have to pass them all. Now as you approach each watch look carefully. If the eyes of all the guards are open and staring straight at you, have no fear. They sleep with their eyes open and they won't see you. But if their eyes are closed, then be careful for when their eyes are closed they are awake and ready to see you. You will find the Grape-Vine in the very center of the garden. Standing near it you will see two spades, a wooden spade and a golden spade. Take the wooden spade and dig up the Vine as quickly as you can. Under no condition touch the golden spade. Now, Janko, do you understand?''

Yes, Janko thought he understood. He slipped into the garden and the first thing he saw were twelve fierce looking guards who were staring at him with great round eyes. He was much frightened until he remembered that the Little Fox had said that if their eyes were open they were fast asleep. So he picked up courage and walked straight by them and sure enough they didn't see him. He passed watch after watch in the same way and at last reached the center of the garden. He saw the Grape-Vine at once. There was no

mistaking it for at that very moment it was pouring
out wine of itself into a golden bucket. Near it were
two spades. Janko in great excitement snatched up the
first that came to his hand and began to dig. Alas,
it was the golden spade and as Janko drove it into the
earth it sent out a loud ringing sound that instantly
woke the guards. They came running from all directions with their eyes tightly closed for now, of course,
they were awake. They caught Janko and dragged him
to the king to whom they said:

"A thief! A thief! We found him trying to steal
your Magic Grape-Vine!"

"My Magic Grape-Vine!" thundered the king.
"Young man, what do you mean trying to steal my
Magic Grape-Vine?"

"Well, you see," Janko answered simply, "the
Grape-Vine really belongs to my father. It was stolen
from him years ago and ever since then his left eye
has wept over the loss of it. Give me the Vine, O
king, for if you don't I shall have to come back and
try again to steal it for it belongs to my father and
I have sworn to get it!"

The king frowned in thought and at last he said:

"I can't give away my precious Grape-Vine for nothing, young man, but I tell you what I'll do: I'll give

it to you provided you get for me the Golden Apple-Tree that bears buds, blossoms, and golden fruit every twenty-four hours."

With that Janko was dismissed and turned out of the garden.

The Little Fox was waiting for him and Janko had the shame of confessing that he had forgotten the warning about the golden spade and had been caught.

"But the king says he will give me the Grape-Vine provided I get for him the Golden Apple-Tree that bears buds, blossoms, and golden fruit every twenty-four hours."

"Well, brother," the Little Fox said, "you were good to me, so I'll help you again. Take hold of my tail and away we'll go."

Janko took hold of the Little Fox's tail and away they went a greater distance than before. In spite of going so quickly it took them a long time but whether it was weeks or months I don't know. Whichever it was when they stopped Janko didn't feel in the least tired or breathless.

"Now, brother," the Little Fox said, "here we are in another country close to the king's garden where the Golden Apple-Tree grows. To reach it you will have to pass twenty-four watches of twelve guards each.

Take care that you pass each guard as before when his eyes are wide open and staring straight at you for that means he is asleep. When you reach the Golden Apple-Tree you will see two long poles on the ground—a wooden pole and a golden pole. Take the wooden pole and beat down some of the golden fruit. Don't touch the golden pole. Remember!"

So Janko crept into the second garden and succeeded in passing all the guards of the twenty-four watches when their eyes were wide open and staring straight at him. He reached the Golden Apple-Tree and saw at once the two long poles that were lying near it on the ground. Now whether because he was excited or because he forgot what the Fox said—he had a good heart, Janko had, but he was a little careless sometimes—I don't know. But I do know that instead of taking the wooden pole as the Fox had told him, he took the golden pole. At the first stroke of the golden pole against the golden branches of the tree, the golden branches sent out a loud clear whistle that woke all the sleeping guards. Every last one of them came running to the Apple-Tree and in no time at all they had captured poor Janko and carried him to their master, the king.

"Trying to steal my Golden Apple-Tree, is he?"

roared the king in a great rage. "What do you want with my Golden Apple-Tree, young man?"

"Well, you see," Janko answered simply, "I have to have the Golden Apple-Tree to exchange it for the Magic Grape-Vine that really belongs to my father. It was stolen from him years ago and ever since then his left eye has wept over the loss of it. Give me the Golden Apple-Tree, O king, for if you don't I shall have to come back and try again to steal it."

The king seemed impressed with Janko's words for after a moment he said:

"Janko, I can't give you the Golden Apple-Tree for nothing, but I tell you what I'll do: I'll let you have it provided you get for me the Golden Horse that can race around the world in twenty-four hours."

With that Janko was dismissed and turned out of the garden.

As usual the Little Fox was waiting for him and again Janko had the shame of confessing that he had forgotten the warning about the golden pole and had been caught.

"But the king says he will give me the Golden Apple-Tree provided I get him the Golden Horse that can race around the world in twenty-four hours. I wonder, dear Little Fox, will you help me again?"

"Yes, brother, I will help you again for you were good to me. Take hold of my tail and away we'll go."

So Janko took hold of the Little Fox's tail and away they went. How far they went and how long they were gone I don't know, but it was a great distance and a long time. However they arrived without feeling in the least tired or breathless.

"Now, brother," the Little Fox said, "this time listen carefully to what I tell you. Here we are in another kingdom close to the king's own stable where the Golden Horse is guarded by thirty-six watches of twelve guards each. When night comes you must slip into the stable and pass all those guards when they are asleep with their eyes wide open and staring straight at you. When you reach the Golden Horse you will see hanging beside him a golden bridle and a common bridle made of hempen rope. Slip the hempen bridle over the Horse's head and lead him quietly out of the stable. But mind you don't touch the golden bridle! This time don't forget!"

Janko promised faithfully to remember what the Little Fox said and when night came he crept into the stable and cautiously made his way through the sleeping guards. He reached at last the stall of the Golden Horse. It was the most beautiful horse in the world and the gleam of its shining flanks was like sunshine in the dark stable.

Janko stroked its golden mane and whispered softly into its ear. The horse responded to his touch and rubbed its muzzle against his shoulder.

Janko reached over to take the hempen bridle and then he paused. " It would be an outrage," he thought to himself, " to put a common rope on this glorious creature! "

Just think of it! For the third time Janko forgot the Little Fox's warning! I have no excuse to make for him. I don't see how he could have forgotten a third time! But he did. He took the golden bridle instead of the hempen one and put it over the head of the Golden Horse. The Horse neighed and instantly all the sleeping guards awoke and came running to the stall. They caught Janko, of course, and when morning broke carried him to their master, the king.

He questioned Janko as the others had done and Janko answered him simply:

" You see I have to have the Golden Horse, O king, to exchange it for the Golden Apple-Tree. And I have to have the Golden Apple-Tree to exchange it for the Magic Grape-Vine that really belongs to my

father. It was stolen from him years ago and ever
since then his left eye has wept over the loss of it.
Give me the Golden Horse, O king, for if you don't
give him to me I shall have to come back and try again
to steal him."

"But, Janko," the king said, "I can't give you the
Golden Horse for nothing! But I tell you what I'll
do: I will give him to you provided you get for me
the Golden Maiden who has never seen the sun."

With that Janko was dismissed and led out of the
stable.

Janko really was awfully ashamed this time when
he had again to confess to the Little Fox that he had
forgotten her warning and had touched the golden
bridle.

"Janko! Janko!" the Little Fox said. "Where
are your wits! Now what shall we do?"

Then Janko told the Little Fox of the king's offer:

"He will give me the Golden Horse provided I get
for him the Golden Maiden who has never seen the sun.
Dear Little Fox, will you help me this one time more?
I know I am very stupid but I promise you faithfully
that this time I will not forget."

"Of course, brother," the Little Fox said, "I'll help
you again. But this will have to be the last time. If

you forget this time I won't be able to help you any more. Take hold of my tail and away we'll go."

So for the fourth time Janko took hold of the Little Fox's tail and away they went. They went and they went—I can't tell you how far! But they weren't tired when they arrived, they weren't even breathless.

"Now, brother," the Little Fox said, "listen carefully to what I tell you. Here we are in another kingdom close to a great cavern where for sixteen years the Golden Maiden has been kept a prisoner under the enchantment of her wicked mother and never allowed to see the golden light of the sun. There are forty-eight chambers in the cavern and each chamber is guarded by a watch of twelve guards. Steal softly through each chamber when the eyes of all the guards are wide open and staring straight at you. In the last chamber of all you will find the Golden Maiden playing in her Golden Cradle. Over the Cradle stands a fearful ghost who will cry out to you to go away and threaten to kill you. But don't be afraid. It is only an empty ghost which the wicked mother has placed there to frighten men off from rescuing the Golden Maiden. Take the Golden Maiden by the hand, put the Golden Cradle on your shoulder, and hurry back to me. But one thing:

As you leave each chamber be sure to lock the door
after you so that the guards when they wake cannot
follow you."

Janko crept into the cavern and cautiously made his
way from chamber to chamber through the wide-eyed
guards. In the forty-eighth chamber he found the
Golden Maiden playing in her Golden Cradle. He ran
to take her when a horrible creature rose above the
Cradle and in hollow tones cried: "Back! Back!
Back!" For a moment Janko was frightened, then
he remembered that the awful creature was only an
empty ghost. So he went boldly up to the Golden
Cradle and sure enough the ghost faded away.

"You have come to rescue me, haven't you?" the
Golden Maiden cried.

She gave Janko her hand and he helped her to her
feet. Then he put the Golden Cradle on his shoulder
and together they hurried out from chamber to chamber. And I am happy to tell you that this time Janko
remembered the Little Fox's warning and locked the
door of every chamber as they left it. So they reached
the upper world safely and found the Little Fox waiting for them.

"There's no time to lose," the Little Fox said. "Put
the Cradle across my back, Janko, and take hold of my

tail with one hand and give your other hand to the
Golden Maiden and away we'll go."

Janko did as the Little Fox said and away they
all three went.

When they reached the stable of the Golden Horse,
the Little Fox said:

" It doesn't seem right to give the Golden Maiden to
the king of the Golden Horse unless she wants us to,
does it? "

The Golden Maiden at once begged them to keep her.

" Don't give me to the king of the Golden Horse! "
she said. " I want to stay with Janko who has rescued
me! "

" But unless I give up the Golden Maiden," Janko
asked, " how can I get the Golden Horse? "

" Perhaps I can help you," the Little Fox said.
" Perhaps I can enchant myself into looking like the
Golden Maiden."

With that the Little Fox leaped up in the air, turned
this way and that, and lo! you might have thought her
the Golden Maiden except that her eyes were still fox's
eyes.

" Now leave the Maiden outside here hidden in her
Golden Cradle and take me in to the master of the
stable. Exchange me for the Golden Horse and make

off at once.   Then pick up the Golden Maiden in her Golden Cradle and ride away and soon I'll join you."

Janko did this very thing. He took in the fox maiden and exchanged her for the Golden Horse and instantly rode off as the Little Fox had told him.

The king of the stable at once called all his courtiers together and showed them the fox maiden.

"See," he said, "this is the Golden Maiden who has never seen the sun! She is the most beautiful maiden in the world and she now belongs to me!"

The courtiers looked at her and admired her, but one of them a little keener than the others said:

"Yes, she's very beautiful and all that but look at her eyes. They don't look like maiden's eyes but like fox's eyes!"

Instantly at the word *fox* the false maiden turned to to a fox and went scampering off.

"See what you've done!" cried the king in a fury. "You have changed my Golden Maiden into a fox with your nonsense! You shall pay for this with your life!" And he had him executed at once.

The Little Fox meantime had caught up with Janko and the Golden Maiden and the Golden Horse. As they neared the garden of the king of the Golden Apple-Tree the Fox said:

" It would be a pity to give away the Golden Horse. Rightly it belongs to the Golden Maiden and was taken from her by her wicked mother."

"Don't give my Golden Horse away!" the Golden Maiden begged.

"But how else can I get the Golden Apple-Tree?" Janko asked.

"Perhaps I can help you," the Little Fox said. "Perhaps I can enchant myself into looking like the Golden Horse."

With that the Little Fox leaped up in the air, turned this way and that, and lo! you might have thought her the Golden Horse except that her tail was still a fox's tail.

When they reached the garden of the Golden Apple-Tree, Janko left the Golden Horse and the Golden Maiden outside and took the fox horse in to the king.

The king was delighted and at once had his servants deliver to Janko the Golden Apple-Tree.

When Janko was safely gone, the king called all his courtiers together and showed them the fox horse.

"See my Golden Horse!" he said. "Isn't it the most beautiful horse in the world!"

"It is! It is!" they all told him.

But one courtier, a little keener than the rest, remarked:

"What a curious tail for a horse to have! It looks like a fox's tail!"

At the word *fox* the false horse changed back into a fox and went scampering off.

"See what you've done with your nonsense!" cried the king. "You have lost me my Golden Horse and now you shall lose your own life!" And he ordered the courtier to be executed at once.

The Fox soon caught up with the real Golden Horse and with Janko and the Golden Maiden who were holding in their arms the Golden Cradle and the Golden Apple-Tree.

"It will never do to give up the Golden Apple-Tree," the Fox said, "for it, too, rightly belongs to the Golden Maiden. I'll have to see again if I can help you."

So when they neared the garden of the Magic Grape-Vine, the Little Fox leaped in the air, turned this way and that, and lo! you might have thought her the Golden Apple-Tree except that her fruit instead of being round was long and pointed like a fox's head.

Janko gave the king the fox tree and received in return the Magic Grape-Vine that really belonged to his

The Golden Maiden, the Farmer and the Empty Ghost

father and not to the king at all. He hurried back to the Golden Maiden who was waiting for him with the Golden Horse and the Golden Apple-Tree and the Golden Cradle and off they all went.

The king was delighted with his fox tree and called his courtiers to come and admire it.

"Beautiful! Beautiful!" they all said, and one of them examining the fruit carefully remarked:

"But see these apples! They are not round like apples but long and pointed like a fox's head!"

He had no sooner said the word *fox* than the tree turned into a fox and went scampering off.

"See what you've done with your nonsense!" cried the king. "You have lost me my Golden Apple-Tree and now I shall lose you your head!" And he ordered the courtier to be executed at once.

When the Fox caught up with the Golden Horse, she said to Janko:

"Now, my brother, it is time for us to part. You have the Magic Grape-Vine and soon your father's left eye will no longer weep. Besides, you are carrying home the Golden Maiden on her own Golden Horse and with her Golden Apple-Tree and her Golden Cradle. God has blessed you in your undertaking and will continue to bless you so long as you are good and kind. Farewell now and think sometimes of your sister, the Little Lame Fox."

Janko wept at thought of parting with the Little Fox and the Little Fox promised him that she would help him again if ever he needed her. Then she turned and trotted off into the woods and Janko rode homewards without her.

When he reached the crossroads where he had parted from his brothers just one year before he came upon a crowd of angry farmers belaboring two men who had been robbing their barns. Janko found that the two men were his own brothers who since he had seen them had fallen into bad company, lost all their money at cards, and had finally taken to thieving. Janko paid the farmers for the damage his brothers had done them and took his brothers home with him.

You can imagine the old farmer's happiness at seeing all three of his sons after a whole year's absence. It was even greater than his delight at getting back his Magic Grape-Vine. But that doesn't mean that he wasn't delighted to have back the Grape-Vine. At the first cup of wine that the Vine poured him, his left eye ceased weeping and it was never known to weep again.

He was delighted, too, at having the Golden Maiden

in the house and pleased when people came from far and near to see the Maiden's Golden Horse and Golden Apple-Tree and Golden Cradle. He even began to hope that she might marry one of his sons before some prince came along and snatched her away. He thought the Maiden would make a wonderful bride for the oldest. Unfortunately Janko had not told him what reprobates the two older sons were, and the older brothers themselves had given their father to understand that it was really they who had found the Magic Grape-Vine and rescued the Golden Maiden. You see instead of being grateful to Janko for having saved their necks from the angry farmers, they hated him worse than ever.

"That Booby!" the older brother growled. "Just because he took the left-hand road and found the Magic Grape-Vine he thinks himself so much better than us! It was just luck—that's all it was! Any one who took the left-hand road could have found the old Grape-Vine!"

"And do you notice the way the Golden Maiden always smiles on him?" the other said. "The first thing we know she'll be marrying him and giving him the Golden Horse and the Golden Apple-Tree and the Golden Cradle! Then where will we be?"

" Brother," whispered the first, " let us make away with him! "

So they plotted together and they asked Janko to go hunting with them the next day. Suspecting nothing Janko went. When they came to a deep well in the woods they asked Janko to reach them a cup of water. As he stooped over into the well they pushed him all the way in and drowned him. That's the kind of brothers they were! Then they went home and pretended to be surprised that Janko hadn't come home before them.

He didn't come that night or the next day either, and the Golden Maiden grew sad and quiet, the Magic Grape-Vine no longer poured out its precious wine every hour, the Golden Apple-Tree stopped putting forth its buds and blossoms and golden fruit, and the Golden Horse languished and drooped its lovely head.

" Everything goes wrong when Janko isn't here! " the farmer said. " Where can he be? "

On the third day the Golden Maiden suddenly began to laugh and sing, the Magic Grape-Vine again poured forth a bucket of precious wine every hour, the Golden Apple-Tree put out buds and blossoms and golden fruit, and the Golden Horse lifted its beautiful head and neighed loud and happily. And do you know why?

Because the Little Lame Fox had just rescued Janko and brought him back to life! She pulled him out of the well, and rolled him about on the ground, and worked over him until all the water was emptied from his lungs and he was able to breathe again.

Then as he opened his eyes the Little Fox said:

" I told you, brother, I'd come again if you needed my help. I was just in time for a little longer and I could never have brought you back to life. And now, brother, the enchantment that held me is broken and I need no longer go about as a Little Lame Fox. My mother was a wicked witch and she enchanted me because she was angry with me for saving a man whom she wanted to kill. So she turned me into a little fox and she said I should have to remain a fox forever unless I succeeded in bringing back to life my benefactor. You are my benefactor, Janko, for you shared your bread and cheese with me the first time we met, and now I have been able to bring you back to life."

As she spoke she changed into a lovely maiden.

" Good-by, Janko," she said. " Go home now and tell your father how your evil brothers have treated you. Unless you do this they will plot against the Golden Maiden and you may not be able to protect her."

So Janko and the maiden kissed each other as a

brother and sister might and the maiden went her way and Janko returned to his father's house.

The Golden Maiden and the old farmer were not in the least surprised to see him for things were so happy again that they just knew it must be because Janko was coming back. But his two brothers when they caught sight of him alive and well were so frightened that they took to their heels and ran off as fast as they could go and what's more they've never shown themselves since. And good riddance, too, I say, for they were wicked evil fellows and would only have injured Janko further if they could.

When Janko told his father all the wicked things they had done, the old farmer could scarcely believe his ears.

"And to think," he said, "I had been hoping the Golden Maiden would marry one of them! Mercy me! Mercy me!"

"But, father," the Golden Maiden said—she called him *father* now and it pleased him mightily; "father, I should rather marry Janko!"

"Marry Janko!" the farmer cried. "Why, my dear, Janko is a stupid lad, not nearly so clever as his two brothers!"

"I don't care if he is stupid. He's got a good heart and that's more than the other two have. And besides that he's got a brave heart for he rescued me from the dark cavern and he faced the awful ghost that stood over my Golden Cradle. Why, father, I'd rather marry Janko than any prince in the world!"

You can imagine Janko's feelings when he heard this!

"I'd feel like a prince if you did marry me, dear Golden One!" he cried.

Well, she did marry him, and sure enough he did feel like a prince. What prince, I'd like to know, had a lovelier bride? None! And was there any prince in the world whose bride brought him greater riches than the Golden Apple-Tree, the Golden Horse, and Golden Cradle? No, not one! And furthermore the farmer promised that, when he died, he would leave him the Magic Grape-Vine.

So Janko lived happy and prosperous. And it all came about through his having a good honest heart.

THE ENCHANTED PEAFOWL

*The Story of the Golden Apples, the Wicked Dragon,
and the Magic Horse*

THE ENCHANTED PEAFOWL

Have you ever heard the story of the Peafowl who became a Queen and of the Tsar's Youngest Son who married her? Well, here it is:

THERE was once a Tsar who took great delight in his garden. Every morning you could see him bending over his flowers or picking the fruit of his favorite tree. This was an apple-tree that had the magic property of bearing buds, blossoms, and golden fruit every twenty-four hours. It was known as the golden apple-tree. In the morning the first thing when he woke up the Tsar would look out his bedroom window to see that all was well with his beloved tree.

One morning when as usual he looked out he was grieved to see that the tree had been stripped of all the golden fruit which had ripened during the night.

"Who has stolen my golden apples?" he cried.

The palace guards looked everywhere for some trace of the thief but found nothing.

The next morning the same thing had happened and

every morning thereafter when the Tsar looked out of his bedroom window he saw that the tree had again been stripped of its golden fruit.

He called his three sons to him and said:

" Is it seemly that a Tsar who has three able-bodied sons should be robbed night after night of his golden apples? Are you willing that this should happen and you do nothing about it? "

The eldest son who was a braggart said:

" My father, you need say no more. I myself will watch to-night and when the thief appears I will overpower him and bring him to you."

So the eldest son watched that night, standing on guard under the apple-tree and leaning against its trunk.

As midnight approached his eyes grew heavy and he fell asleep. While he slept the golden apples ripened and were stolen and the next morning, as usual, the branches were bare.

The second son who was a crafty youth laughed at his brother and said:

" To-night I will watch. I will pretend to be asleep and when the thief appears I will jump upon him and overpower him."

So when night came the second son went on guard

under the tree and in order to deceive the thief he
lay down on the ground and closed his eyes. At first
he stayed wide awake but as the hours dragged by he
grew tired and then, because he was in such a comfortable position, he too fell soundly asleep. Midnight
came and the apples ripened but the next morning,
when the second prince awoke, the tree had again been
stripped of its golden fruit.

The Tsar's Youngest Son now said:

" Father, let me go on guard to-night."

His brothers jeered and the Tsar shook his head.

" Nay, nay, my boy, why should you succeed where
your older brothers have failed? It is God's will that
my golden apples should be stolen and I must sub-
mit."

But the Youngest Son insisted that he, too, be given
a chance to capture the thief and at last the Tsar consented.

" I will sleep soundly the first part of the night,"
the Youngest Prince thought to himself, " and with
God's help wake up at midnight."

As soon as it was dark he had his bed carried outdoors and placed under the apple-tree. Then after
commending his undertaking to God he lay down and
fell soundly to sleep. Just before midnight he awoke.

The apples had ripened and were shining among the leaves like golden lanterns.

On the stroke of midnight there was a whirr of wings and nine beautiful peafowl came flying down from the sky. Eight of them settled on the branches of the apple-tree and began eating the golden fruit. The ninth alighted beside the Young Prince and as she touched the ground changed into a lovely maiden.

She was so beautiful and gentle that the Young Prince fell madly in love with her and at once began wooing her with kisses and caresses. She responded to his love and they spent the night together in great happiness.

At the first streak of dawn she jumped up, saying:

"My dear one, I must leave you now!"

"But you will come again, won't you?" the Prince asked.

"Yes," she promised him. "To-night."

Suddenly the Prince remembered the golden apples. The peafowl in the tree were about to eat the last of them.

"Can't you make them leave just one apple for my father?" the Prince begged.

The maiden spoke to the birds and they flew down

with two of the golden apples, one for the Tsar and one for the Prince himself.

Then the maiden lifted her arms above her head, changed into a peafowl, and with the other eight flew off into the morning sky.

The Prince carried the two apples to his father and the Tsar was so delighted that he forgot to ask the Prince the particulars of his adventure.

The next night the Prince again slept under the apple-tree and awoke just before midnight to hear the whirr of wings and see the nine peafowl come flying down from the sky. Eight of them settled on the branches of the apple-tree and the ninth, as before, alighted beside him and as she touched the earth changed into the lovely maiden of his heart. Again they passed the night together in great happiness and in the early dawn before she flew away the maiden gave him the last two of the golden apples.

This went on night after night until the Prince's two elder brothers were mad with jealousy and consumed with curiosity to know what happened every night under the apple-tree. At last they went to an evil old woman and bribed her to spy on the Young Prince.

"Find out what happens every night at the apple-tree," they told her, "and we will reward you richly."

So the evil old woman hid herself near the apple-tree and that night when the prince fell asleep she crept under his bed. Midnight came and she heard the whirr of wings and presently she saw the white feet of a lovely maiden touch the ground and she heard the prince say: " My love, is it you? "

Then as the Prince and the maiden began kissing each other and exchanging vows of love very slowly and cautiously she reached up her hand from under the bed and groped around until she felt the maiden's hair. Then with a scissors she snipped off a lock.

" Oh! " the maiden cried in terror. She jumped up, lifted her arms above her head, changed into a peafowl, and without another word flew off with the other eight and vanished in the sky.

In a fury the Prince searched about to see what had frightened his loved one. He found the old woman under the bed and dragging her out by the hair he struck her dead with his sword. And good riddance it was, too, for she was an evil old thing and only caused mischief in the world.

But putting the evil old woman out of the way did not, alas, bring back the lovely maiden. The Prince waited for her the next night and the next and many following nights but she nevermore returned.

The magic apple-tree of course was no longer robbed of its golden fruit, so the Tsar was happy once again and never tired of praising the valor of his youngest son. But as for the prince, in spite of his father's praise he grew sadder and sadder.

Finally he went to the Tsar and said:

"Father, I have lost the maiden whom I love and life without her is not worth the living. Unless I go out in the world and find her I shall die."

The Tsar tried to dissuade him but when he could not he mounted him on a fine horse, gave him a serving man to accompany him, and sent him off with his blessing.

The Prince and his man wandered hither and thither over the world inquiring everywhere for news of nine peafowl one of whom was a lovely maiden. They came at last to a lake on the shore of which lived an ugly old woman with an only daughter.

"Nine peafowl," she repeated, "and one of them a lovely maiden! You must mean the nine sisters, the enchanted princesses, who fly about as peafowl. They come here every morning to bathe in the lake. What can you want with them?"

The Prince told the old woman that one of them

was his love and that unless he married her he would die.

"Die, indeed!" scoffed the old woman. "That's no way for a handsome young man to talk! I'll tell you what you ought to do: give up thought of this peafowl princess and marry my daughter. Then I'll make you heir to all my riches."

She called out her daughter who was as ugly as herself and cross and ill-natured in the bargain. Just one look at her and the Prince said firmly:

"No! If I can't marry my own dear love I won't marry any one!"

"Very well!" said the old woman shortly.

When the Prince's back was turned she called the serving man aside and whispered:

"Will you do what I tell you if I pay you well?"

The serving man who was a mean greedy fellow nodded his head and the old woman handed him a small bellows.

"Hide this in your shirt," she told him, "and don't let your master see it. Then to-morrow morning when you go down to the lake with him to see the nine peafowl slip it out and blow it on the back of his neck. Do this and I'll give you a golden ducat."

The serving man took the bellows and did as the old

woman directed. The next morning down at the lake just as the nine peafowl came flying into sight he crept up behind the Prince and blew the bellows on the back of his neck. Instantly sleep overcame the Prince. His eyes closed, his head drooped, and the reins fell from his hands.

Eight of the peafowl alighted on the water's edge, changed into lovely maidens and went bathing in the lake, but the ninth flew straight down to the Prince, fluttered her wings in his face and uttering sad cries tried hard to arouse him.

The eight finished their baths, changed back into birds, and calling their sister they all flew off together. Then and not till then did the Prince awaken.

"Ah!" he cried, "how could I have fallen asleep just when the peafowl appeared? Where are they now? Are they gone?"

"Yes," his man told him, "they're gone. Eight of them changed into lovely maidens and went bathing in the lake but the ninth fluttered about your head and tried in every way to arouse you. I tried to arouse you, too, but you kept on sleeping."

"Strange!" thought the Prince. "How could I have fallen asleep at such a time? I'll have to try again to-morrow morning."

The next morning the same thing happened. The treacherous serving man again blew the bellows on the back of the Prince's neck and instantly the Prince sank into a deep sleep from which the ninth peafowl was unable to arouse him.

As she rose to join her sisters she said to the serving man:

"When your master awakens tell him that to-morrow is the last day we shall come here to bathe in the lake."

The peafowl were no sooner gone than the Prince rubbed his eyes and looked about.

"What! Where are they? Have I been asleep again?"

The serving man pretended to be deeply grieved.

"I tried hard to awaken you, master, but I couldn't. The ninth peafowl as she flew away said to tell you that to-morrow is the last day they'll come to the lake."

The next day as the Prince waited for the appearance of the nine peafowl he galloped madly along the shore of the lake hoping in this way to ward off the strange sleep. But the moment the nine peafowl appeared in the sky he was so delighted that he drew rein and the treacherous serving man was able to slip up behind him and blow the magic bellows on his neck.

So again he slept soundly while the ninth peafowl fluttered about his head and tried vainly to arouse him.

As she was flying away she said to the serving man:

"Tell your master that now he will never find me unless he strikes off the head from the nail."

When the Prince awoke the serving man delivered this message.

"What can she mean?" the Prince said.

He looked hard at the serving man and something in the fellow's appearance made him suspect treachery.

"You know more than you're telling me!" the Prince cried, and taking the cowardly fellow by the throat he shook him and choked him until he had got the truth out of him.

"Ha!" cried the Prince. "Now I understand! You are the nail of which my dear love warns me!"

The fellow whined and begged for mercy but the Prince with one blow of his sword struck off his head. Then, leaving the body where it fell for the old woman to bury, he mounted his horse and again set forth on his quest.

Everywhere he went he made inquiries about the nine enchanted peafowl and everywhere people shook their heads and said they had never heard of them. At last high up in a wild mountain he found an old hermit who knew all about them.

"Ah," he said, "you mean the nine princesses. Eight of them have broken the enchantment that held them and are now happily married. The ninth awaits you. She is living in the royal palace of a beautiful city that lies three days' journey to the north of this mountain. When you find her, if you do just as she says she, too, will soon be free of all enchantment. Then she will be made queen."

The Prince thanked the hermit and rode on. After three days he came to the city of which the hermit had told him. He made his way to the palace and into the Princess's presence. Sure enough the Princess was his own dear love. She received him with joy, promised soon to marry him, and gave over to him the keys of the palace.

"You shall now be master here," she told him, "to go where you like and do as you like. There is only one thing that you must not do, only one place where you must not go. Under the palace are twelve cellars. Here are the keys to them all. Go into eleven of them whenever you will but you must never open the door of the twelfth one. If you do a heavy misfortune may fall upon both of us."

One day while the Princess was walking in the garden, the young Prince thought he would go through the cellars. So, taking the keys, he unlocked the cellars one after another until he had seen eleven of them. Then he stood before the door of the twelfth wondering why the Princess had warned him not to open it.

"I'll open it just a little," he thought to himself. "If there's something inside that tries to get out, I'll close it quickly."

So he took the twelfth key, unlocked the twelfth door, and peeped inside the twelfth cellar. It was empty except for one huge cask with an open bunghole.

"I don't see anything in here to be afraid of," he said.

Just then he heard a groan from inside the cask and a voice called out in a begging, whining tone:

"A cup of water, brother! A cup of water! I am dying of thirst!"

Now the Prince thought to himself that it was a terrible thing for any living creature to be dying of thirst. So he hurried out, got a cup of water, and poured it into the open bunghole. Instantly one of the three iron hoops that bound the cask burst asunder and the voice inside the cask said:

"Thank you, brother! Thank you! Now give me another cup! I am dying of thirst!"

So the Prince poured in a second cup and the second iron hoop snapped apart and when the voice still begged for more water he poured in a third cup. The third hoop broke, the staves of the cask fell in, and a horrid dragon sprang out. Before the Prince could move, he had flown through the door of the twelfth cellar into the eleventh cellar, then into the tenth cellar, the ninth cellar, the eight cellar, the seventh cellar, the sixth, the fifth, the fourth, the third, the second, the first, and so out into the garden. The Prince reached the garden just in time to see the monster overpower the Princess.

"Alas, my dear one, what have you done?" cried the poor Princess as the dragon carried her off. "The enchantment would soon have been broken and I could have married you if only you had not gone into the twelfth cellar!"

Heartbroken at what had happened, the Prince mounted his horse and started off in pursuit of the dragon.

"I must do what I can to rescue my loved one," he said, "even if it costs me my life."

He rode many days until he came to the castle of

the dragon. The dragon was out and the Princess received him with tears of joy.

" Come," he said to her, " let us escape before the dragon returns."

The Princess sighed and shook her head.

" How, my loved one, can we escape? The dragon rides a magic horse and however fast we go he will be able to overtake us."

But the Prince insisted that they make the attempt. So she mounted with him and off they went.

When the dragon arrived home and found her gone, he laughed a brutal laugh and said to his horse:

" I suppose that foolish young Prince has been here and is trying to carry her off. Shall we start after them now or wait till we've had our supper? "

" We might as well eat," the horse said, " for we'll overtake them anyway."

So they both ate and then the dragon mounted the magic horse and in no time at all they had overtaken the fugitives.

" I ought to tear you to pieces," the dragon said to the Prince, " but I won't this time because you gave me a cup of water. However, I warn you not to try this foolishness again! "

With that he clutched the poor weeping Princess in his scaly arms and carried her back to the castle.

What was the Prince to do now? He tried to plan some other way of rescuing the Princess but he could think of none. In spite of the dragon's threat he went back the next day and tried the same thing again. Again the dragon overtook him and snatched back the Princess.

" I have spared you one time," he said to the Prince, " and I will spare you this one time more for the sake of the water you gave me. But I warn you if you come again I will tear you to pieces."

But what man worthy the name will accept such a warning when the safety and happiness of his loved one is concerned? The next day while the dragon was out the Prince again returned to the castle.

" It is plain," he said to the Princess, " that we can never escape until we, too, get a magic horse. We must find out where the dragon got his. To-night when he comes home, speak him fair and caress his head and when he is in fine humor ask him about his horse—what kind of a horse it is and where he got it. Then I will come back to-morrow at this same hour and you can tell me."

So that night when the dragon came home the Prin-

cess allowed him to put his head in her lap and she
scratched him softly behind the ears and petted him
until he was purring like a giant cat.

"Urrh! Urrh! Urrh!" purred the dragon. "How
happy we are here, just you and I! What a foolish
young man that Prince of yours is to think I'd let him
carry you off! Urrh! Urrh! Urrh!"

"Yes," the Princess agreed, "he is foolish or he
would never suppose his horse could outrace yours."

"Urrh! Urrh!" the dragon purred. "You're right!
He seems to think my horse is an ordinary horse. Why,
I got my horse from the Old Woman of the Mountain
and the only other horse in the world that can out-
strip him is another horse that the Old Woman still
has. The Prince would have a hard time getting
him!"

The Princess still scratching the dragon behind his
ears, just where he loved it most, asked softly:

"Why?"

"Urrh! Urrh! Urrh! Because the Old Woman
will never give that horse away until a man comes along
who is able to guard for three nights in succession the
Old Woman's mare and foal. Any one who attempts
this and fails she kills. But even if a man were to succeed he would never get the right horse for the old

witch would palm off another on him. Urrh! Urrh! Urrh! Oh, that feels good, my dear!"

"How would she do that?" the Princess asked.

"Urrh! Urrh! Urrh! You see she says to every man who undertakes to guard the mare: 'If you suc- ceed you may have any horse in my stable.' Then she shows him twelve beautiful stallions with shiny coats, but she doesn't show him a scrawny miserable looking beast that lies neglected on the dung heap. Yet this is the magic horse and brother to mine."

Now the Princess knew all she needed to know and the next day when the Prince came she told him what the dragon had said. So the Prince at once set out to find the Old Woman of the Mountain.

He traveled three days over waste places and through strange lands. On the first day as he was riding along the shores of a lake he heard a little voice crying out:

"Help me, brother, help me and—who knows?— some day I may help you!"

The Prince looked down and saw a fish that was floundering on the sand. He dismounted to get the fish and throw it back into the water.

"Take one of my scales," the fish said. "Then if ever you need my help just rub the scale."

So the Prince, before he threw the fish into the lake,

scraped off a scale and tied it in a corner of his hand-kerchief. Then he rode on.

The second day a fox that had been caught in a trap called out to him:

"Help me, brother, help me and—who knows?—some day I may help you!"

The Prince opened the trap and the fox, before it limped away, gave the Prince one of its hairs and said:

"If ever you need me, rub this hair."

The third day he met a raven that had fallen on a thorn and was pinned to the ground.

"Help me, brother, help me!" the raven begged, "and—who knows?—some day I may help you!"

The Prince lifted the raven off the thorn and the raven, before it flew away, gave the Prince one of its feathers saying:

"If ever you need me, rub this feather."

So the Prince reached the house of the Old Woman of the Mountain with the fish's scale, the fox's hair, and the raven's feather each safely tied in a corner of his handkerchief.

The Old Woman of the Mountain was an ugly old witch with a long nose that hooked down and a long chin that hooked up.

"Ha! Ha!" she cackled when she saw the Prince.

"Another one that wants service with the Old Woman, eh?"

"Yes," said the Prince.

"You know the conditions?" the Old Woman said. "Guard my mare and her foal for three nights in succession and you may have any horse in my stable. But if she escapes you, then your head is mine and I'll stick it up there as a warning to other rash young men."

The Old Woman pointed to a high picket fence that surrounded the courtyard. On every picket but one there was a grinning human skull. The Prince looked and the only picket that had no skull called out:

"I want my skull, granny! I want my skull!"

The Old Woman gave a wicked laugh.

"You see," she said, "we were expecting you!"

When night fell the Prince led out the mare and her foal to a grassy meadow. To make sure that she would not escape him, he mounted her. Midnight came and he must have fallen asleep for suddenly he awoke to find himself astride a rail with an empty bridle in his hand. In despair he looked in all directions. At one end of the meadow was a pond.

"She may have gone there to drink," he said to himself.

At the pond he saw a hoofprint.

The Old Woman of the Mountain and the Wonder Horse

"Ah," he thought, "if my fish were here, it could tell me."

He untied the corner of the hankerchief that had the fish scale, rubbed the scale gently, and at once a little voice called out from the water:

"What is it, brother? Can I help you?"

"Can you tell me what has become of the Old Woman's mare and foal?"

"Aye, brother, that I can! She and the foal are turned into fish and are down here in the water hiding amongst us. Strike the water three times with the bridle and say: 'Mare of the Old Woman, come out!' That will bring her!"

The Prince did this. There was a commotion in the water, a big fish and a little fish leaped high in the air, fell on shore, and instantly changed to mare and foal. When morning came the Prince drove them back to the Old Woman.

She grinned and pretended to be pleased but, when she had the mare alone in the stable, the Prince heard her beating the poor creature and saying:

"Why didn't you do as I told you and hide among the fishes?"

"I did," whinnied the mare, "but the fishes are his friends and he found me!"

"To-night," the Old Woman snarled, "hide among the foxes and this time don't let him find you! Do you hear me? The foxes!"

The Prince remembered this and the second night when he awoke to find himself again sitting astride a rail and holding an empty bridle in his hand, he untied the second corner of his handkerchief, took out the fox's hair, and rubbed it gently.

Instantly he heard a little bark and the fox's voice said:

"What is it, brother? Can I help you?"

"Can you tell me," the Prince asked, "what has become of the Old Woman's mare and foal?"

"Aye, brother, that I can! She and the foal are turned into foxes and are over in yonder woods now hiding among my people. Strike the earth three times with the bridle and say: 'Mare of the Old Woman, come back!' That will bring her!"

The Prince did this and instantly two foxes, a vixen and a cub, came trotting out of the woods and when they reached the Prince they changed back to mare and foal.

In the morning the Prince drove them home to the Old Woman. As before she grinned and pretended to be pleased but when she had the mare alone in the stable the Prince heard her giving the poor creature another beating and saying:

" Why didn't you do as I told you and hide among the foxes? "

" I did," whinnied the mare, " but the foxes are his friends, too, and he found me! "

" To-night," the Old Woman ordered, " hide among the ravens and this time don't let him find you! "

The third night the Prince tried hard to stay awake but sleep again overcame him and when he woke he found himself for the third time sitting astride a rail and holding the empty bridle in his hand. But he remembered the Old Woman's words and at once opened the third corner of his handkerchief and taking out the raven's feather rubbed it gently.

There was a flutter of wings and a raven's hoarse voice said:

" Caw! Caw! What is it, brother? Can I help you? "

" Can you tell me what has become of the Old Woman's mare and foal? "

" Aye, brother, that I can! She and the foal are turned into ravens and are perched in yonder tall fir tree hiding among my folk. Strike the trunk of the tree three times with your bridle and say: ' Mare of

the Old Woman, come down!' That will bring
her!'"

The Prince went over to the fir tree, struck it three
times with the bridle and said:

"Mare of the Old Woman, come down!"

Instantly two ravens, a big one and a fledgling, fluttered to earth and changed to mare and foal. So when
morning came the Prince was able to drive them back
to the Old Woman and claim his reward.

The Old Woman was angry enough to kill him but
she pretended to be pleased and she smiled and grinned
and she patted the Prince on the arm and said:

"Aye, my son, but you are a hero! You have won
the reward and you are worthy of it. Choose now the
finest horse in my stable. It is yours."

She drove the twelve handsome stallions out into the
courtyard and urged them on the Prince one after the
other. But at each the Prince shook his head.

"I am only a poor adventurer," he said. "Such
horses as these are too fine for me. Give me rather
that poor mangy creature that lies over yonder on the
dung heap. That is the one I choose."

Then the Old Woman fell into an awful rage and
shook and chattered and begged the Prince not to take
that horse.

"It would shame me," she said, "to have you ride off on that poor beast which is half dead already! No, no, my son, you mustn't take him!"

"But that's the one I'm going to take," the Prince said firmly, "that and none other!" He drew his sword and lifted it threateningly. "I have won whatever horse I choose and now, Old Woman, if you do not keep your bargain I shall strike you dead with this sword and stick up your grinning skull on that empty picket!"

At that the empty picket began to shout:

"I want my skull! I want my skull!"

When the Old Woman of the Mountain saw that the Prince knew what he was about, she gave up trying to deceive him and let him lead off the horse he wanted. So the Prince walked away dragging the poor mangy creature after him. When he was out of sight of the Old Woman's house, he turned to the horse and began rubbing down his rough coat and patting his wobbly legs.

"Now, my beauty," he said, "we'll see what you're made of!"

Under his hand the mangy beast changed to a glorious animal—one of those wonder horses of the olden days that rise on the wind and gallop with the clouds.

Soon his coat shone like burnished gold and his tail and mane streamed out like flames of fire.

"Ah, my master," the horse said, "I have been waiting for you this many a day! We shall have glorious adventures together!"

Then the Prince mounted him and he rose on the wind and went so swiftly that he covered in three minutes all the distance that it had taken the Prince three days to go on an ordinary horse. Whiff! and there they were at the dragon's castle and there was the Princess running out to welcome them.

"Now, my dear one," the Prince said, lifting the Princess up in front of him, "this time the dragon will not overtake us!"

The wonder horse rose on the wind and off they went.

When the dragon got home and found that the Princess had fled again, he said to his horse:

"Shall we follow her at once or shall we eat supper first?"

"It's all one what we do," the horse said, "for we shall never overtake her."

At that the dragon leaped upon his horse and, mounting on the wind, started off in hot pursuit. Presently they caught sight of the other horse carrying the Prince and the Princess but, try as he would, the dragon's horse could not overtake the other. The dragon beat his horse unmercifully and dug his sharp claws into the horse's tender flanks until the horse in agony called out to the Prince's horse:

"Hold, brother, hold! Let me overtake you or this monster will kill me with his cruelty!"

"Why do you carry such a monster?" the Prince's horse called back. "Throw him from you and be rid of him forever!"

At that the dragon's horse reared suddenly and the dragon, losing his balance, fell and was dashed to pieces on the rocks below.

And that was the end of that dragon!

Then the Princess wept but her tears were tears of joy for she knew now that the enchantment that had bound her was broken forever. Never again would she be changed into a peafowl at the whim of a wicked dragon, never again be separated from her loved one. Presently she mounted the dragon's horse and together she and the Prince returned to the beautiful city. The people came out to meet them and when they heard of the dragon's death a holiday was proclaimed and amidst music and dancing and merrymaking the Princess married the Prince. Then she was made Queen of that beautiful city and the Prince was made King. They ruled long and wisely and better than that they lived happily for they loved each other.

So now you know the story of the Peafowl who became a Queen and of the Tsar's Youngest Son who married her.

THE DRAGON'S STRENGTH

The Story of the Youngest Prince Who Killed the Sparrow

THE DRAGON'S STRENGTH

THERE was once a King who had three sons. One day the oldest son went hunting and when night fell his huntsmen came riding home without him.

" Where is the prince? " the King asked.

" Isn't he here? " the huntsmen said. " He left us in midafternoon chasing a hare near the Old Mill up the river. We haven't seen him since and we supposed he must have come home alone."

When he hadn't returned the following day his brother, the second prince, went out to search for him.

" I'll go to the Old Mill," he said to the King, " and see what's become of him."

So he mounted his horse and rode up the river. As he neared the Old Mill a hare crossed his path and the second prince being a hunter like his brother at once gave chase. His attendant waited for his return but waited in vain. Night fell and still there was no sign of the second prince.

The attendant returned to the palace and told the King what had happened. The King was surprised but not unduly alarmed and the following day when the

Youngest Prince asked to go hunting alone the King
suggested that he go in the direction of the Old Mill
to find out if he could what was keeping his brothers.

The Youngest Prince who had listened carefully to
what his brothers' attendants had reported decided to
act cautiously. So when a hare crossed his path as he
approached the Old Mill, instead of giving it chase, he
rode off as though he were hunting other game. Later
he returned to the Old Mill from another direction.

He found an old woman sitting in front of it.

"Good evening, granny," he said in a friendly tone,
pulling up his horse for a moment's chat. "Do you
live here? You know I thought the Old Mill was deserted."

The old woman looked at him and shook her head
gloomily.

"Deserted indeed! My boy, take an old woman's
advice and don't have anything to do with this old mill!
It's an evil place!"

"Why, granny," the Prince said, "what's the matter
with it?"

The old woman peered cautiously around and when
she saw they were alone she beckoned the Prince to
come near. Then she whispered:

"A dragon lives here! A horrible monster! He

takes the form of a hare and lures people into the mill. Then he captures them. Some of them he kills and eats and others he holds as prisoners in an underground dungeon. I'm one of his prisoners and he keeps me here to work for him."

"Granny," the Youngest Prince said, "would you like me to rescue you?"

"My boy, you couldn't do it! You have no idea what a strong evil monster the dragon is."

"If you found out something for me, granny, I think I might be able to overcome the dragon and rescue you."

The old woman was doubtful but she promised to do anything the Youngest Prince asked.

"Well then, granny, find out from the dragon where his strength is, whether in his own body or somewhere else. Find out to-night and I'll come back to-morrow at this same hour to see you."

So that night when the dragon came home, after he had supped and when she was scratching his head to make him drowsy for bed, the old woman said to him:

"Master, I think you're the strongest dragon in the world! Tell me now, where does your strength lie— in your own beautiful body or somewhere else?"

"You're right, old woman," the dragon grunted: "I

am pretty strong as dragons go. But I don't keep my
strength in my own body. No, indeed! That would
be too dangerous. I keep it in the hearth yonder."

At that the old woman ran over to the hearth and,
stooping down, she kissed it and caressed it.

" O beautiful hearth! " she said, " where my master's
strength is hidden! How happy are the ashes that
cover your stones! "

The dragon laughed with amusement.

" That's the time I fooled you, old woman! My
strength isn't in the hearth at all! It's in the tree in
front of the mill."

The old woman at once ran out of the mill and threw
her arms about the tree.

" O tree! " she cried, " most beautiful tree in the
world, guard carefully our master's strength and let no
harm come to it! "

Again the dragon laughed.

" I've fooled you another time, old woman! Come
here and scratch my head some more and this time
I'll tell you the truth for I see you really love your
master."

So the old woman went back and scratched the
dragon's head and the dragon told her the truth about
his strength.

"I keep it far away," he said. "In the third kingdom from here near the Tsar's own city there is a deep lake. A dragon lives at the bottom of the lake. In the dragon there is a wild boar; in the boar a hare; in the hare a pigeon; in the pigeon a sparrow. My strength is in the sparrow. Let any one kill the sparrow and I should die that instant. But I am safe. No one but shepherds ever come to the lake and even they don't come any more for the dragon has eaten up so many of them that the lake has got a bad name. Indeed, nowadays even the Tsar himself is hard put to it to find a shepherd. Oh, I tell you, old woman, your master is a clever one!"

So now the old woman had the dragon's secret and the next day she told it to the Youngest Prince. He at once devised a plan whereby he hoped to overcome the dragon. He dressed himself as a shepherd and with crook in hand started off on foot for the third kingdom. He traveled through villages and towns, across rivers and over mountains, and reached at last the third kingdom and the Tsar's own city. He presented himself at the palace and asked employment as a shepherd.

The guards looked at him in surprise and said:

"A shepherd! Are you sure you want to be a shepherd?"

Then they called to their companions: " Here's a youth who wants to be a shepherd! " And the word went through the palace and even the Tsar heard it.

" Send the youth to me," he ordered.

" Do you really want to be my shepherd? " he asked the Youngest Prince.

The Youngest Prince said yes, he did.

" If I put you in charge of the sheep, where would you pasture them? "

" Isn't there a lake beyond the city," the Prince asked, " where the grazing is good? "

" H'm! " said the Tsar. " So you know about that lake, too! What else do you know? "

" I've heard the shepherds disappear."

" And still you want to try your luck? " the Tsar exclaimed.

Just then the Tsar's only daughter, a lovely Princess, who had been looking at the young stranger, slipped over to her father and whispered:

" But, father, you can't let such a handsome young man as that go off with the sheep! It would be dreadful if he never returned! "

The Tsar whispered back:

" Hush, child! Your concern for the young man's safety does credit to your noble feelings. But this is not the time or the place for sentiment. We must consider first the welfare of the royal sheep."

He turned to the Youngest Prince:

"Very well, young man, you may consider yourself engaged as shepherd. Provide yourself with whatever you need and assume your duties at once."

"There is one thing," the Youngest Prince said; "when I start out to-morrow morning with the sheep I should like to take with me two strong boarhounds, a falcon, and a set of bagpipes."

"You shall have them all," the Tsar promised.

Early the next morning when the Princess peeped out of her bedroom window she saw the new shepherd driving the royal flocks to pasture. A falcon was perched on his shoulder; he had a set of bagpipes under his arm; and he was leading two powerful boarhounds on a leash.

"It's a shame!" the Princess said to herself. "He'll probably never return and he's such a handsome young man, too!" And she was so unhappy at thought of never again seeing the new shepherd that she couldn't go back to sleep.

Well, the Youngest Prince reached the lake and turned out his sheep to graze. He perched the falcon on a log, tied the dogs beside it, and laid his bagpipes

on the ground. Then he took off his smock, rolled up
his hose, and wading boldly into the lake called out in
a loud voice:

"Ho, dragon, come out and we'll try a wrestling
match! That is, if you're not afraid!"

"Afraid?" bellowed an awful voice. "Who's
afraid?"

The water of the lake churned this way and that and
a horrible scaly monster came to the surface. He
crawled out on shore and clutched the Prince around
the waist. And the Prince clutched him in a grip just
as strong and there they swayed back and forth, and
rolled over, and wrestled together on the shore of the
lake without either getting the better of the other. By
midafternoon when the sun was hot, the dragon grew
faint and cried out:

"Oh, if I could but dip my burning head in the cool
water, then I could toss you as high as the sky!"

"Don't talk nonsense!" the Prince said. "If the
Tsar's daughter would kiss my forehead, then I could
toss you twice as high!"

After that the dragon slipped out of the Prince's
grasp, plunged into the water, and disappeared. The
Prince waited for him but he didn't show his scaly head
again that day.

When evening came, the Prince washed off the grime of the fight, dressed himself carefully, and then looking as fresh and handsome as ever drove home his sheep. With the falcon on his shoulder and the two hounds at his heels he came playing a merry tune on his bagpipes.

The townspeople hearing the bagpipes ran out of their houses and cried to each other:

" The shepherd's come back! "

The Princess ran to her window and, when she saw the shepherd alive and well, she put her hand to her heart and said:

" Oh! "

Even the Tsar was pleased.

" I'm not a bit surprised that he's back! " he said. " There's something about this youth that I like! "

The next day the Tsar sent two of his trusted servants to the lake to see what was happening there. They hid themselves behind some bushes on a little hill that commanded the lake. They were there when the shepherd arrived and they watched him as he waded out into the water and challenged the dragon as on the day before.

They heard the shepherd call out in a loud voice:

" Ho, dragon, come out and we'll try a wrestling match! That is, if you're not afraid! "

And from the water they heard an awful voice bellow back:

" Afraid? Who's afraid? "

Then they saw the water of the lake churn this way and that and a horrible scaly monster come to the surface. They saw him crawl out on shore and clutch the shepherd around the waist. And they saw the shepherd clutch him in a grip just as strong. And they watched the two as they swayed back and forth and rolled over and wrestled together without either getting the better of the other. By midafternoon when the sun grew hot they saw the dragon grow faint and they heard him cry out:

" Oh, if I could only dip my burning head in the cool water, then I could toss you as high as the sky! "

And they heard the shepherd reply:

" Don't talk nonsense! If the Tsar's daughter would kiss my forehead, then I could toss you twice as high! "

Then they saw the dragon slip out of the shepherd's grasp, plunge into the water, and disappear. They waited but he didn't show his scaly head again that day.

So the Tsar's servants hurried home before the shepherd and told the Tsar all they had seen and heard. The Tsar was mightily impressed with the bravery of the shepherd and he declared that if he killed that horrid dragon he should have the Princess herself for wife!

He sent for his daughter and told her all that his servants had reported and he said to her:

" My daughter, you, too, can help rid your country of this monster if you go out with the shepherd tomorrow and when the time comes kiss him on the forehead. You will do this, will you not, for your country's sake? "

The Princess blushed and trembled and the Tsar, looking at her in surprise, said:

" What! Shall a humble shepherd face a dragon unafraid and the daughter of the Tsar tremble! "

" Father," the Princess cried, " it isn't the dragon that I'm afraid of! "

" What then? " the Tsar asked.

But what it was she was afraid of the Princess would not confess. Instead she said:

" If the welfare of my country require that I kiss the shepherd on the forehead, I shall do so."

So the next morning when the shepherd started out with his sheep, the falcon on his shoulder, the dogs at his heels, the bagpipes under his arm, the Princess walked beside him.

Her eyes were downcast and he saw that she was trembling.

"Do not be afraid, dear Princess," he said to her. "Nothing shall harm you—I promise that!"

"I'm not afraid," the Princess murmured. But she continued to blush and tremble and, although the shepherd tried to look into her eyes to reassure her, she kept her head averted.

This time the Tsar himself and many of his courtiers had gone on before and taken their stand on the hill that overlooked the lake to see the final combat of the shepherd and the dragon.

When the shepherd and the Princess reached the lake, the shepherd put his falcon on the log as before and tied the dogs beside it and laid his bagpipes on the ground. Then he threw off his smock, rolled up his hose, and wading boldly into the lake called out in a loud voice:

"Ho, dragon, come out and we'll try a wrestling match! That is, if you're not afraid!"

"Afraid?" bellowed an awful voice. "Who's afraid?"

The water of the lake churned this way and that and the horrible scaly monster came to the surface. He crawled to shore and clutched the shepherd around the

Next Morning the Princess Peeped Out and Saw the Shepherd

waist. The shepherd clutched him in a grip just as strong and there they swayed back and forth and rolled over and wrestled together on the shore of the lake without either getting the better of the other. The Princess without the least show of fear stood nearby calling out encouragement to the shepherd and waiting for the moment when the shepherd should need her help.

By midafternoon when the sun was hot, the dragon grew faint and cried out:

" Oh, if I could but dip my burning head in the cool water, then I could toss you as high as the sky! "

" Don't talk nonsense! " the shepherd said. " If the Tsar's daughter would kiss my forehead then I could toss you twice as high! "

Instantly the Princess ran forward and kissed the shepherd three times. The first kiss fell on his forehead, the second on his nose, the third on his mouth. With each kiss his strength increased an hundredfold and taking the dragon in a mighty grip he tossed him up so high that for a moment the Tsar and all the courtiers lost sight of him in the sky. Then he fell to earth with such a thud that he burst.

Out of his body sprang a wild boar. The shepherd was ready for this and on the moment he unleashed the two hounds and they fell on the boar and tore him to pieces.

Out of the boar jumped a rabbit. It went leaping across the meadow but the dogs caught it and killed it.

Out of the rabbit flew a pigeon. Instantly the shepherd unloosed the falcon. It rose high in the air, then swooped down upon the pigeon, clutched it in its talons, and delivered it into the shepherd's hands.

He cut open the pigeon and found the sparrow.

" Spare me! Spare me! " squawked the sparrow.

" Tell me where my brothers are," the shepherd demanded with his fingers about the sparrow's throat.

" Your brothers? They are alive and in the deep dungeon that lies below the Old Mill. Behind the mill there are three willow saplings growing from one old root. Cut the saplings and strike the root. A heavy iron door leading down into the dungeon will open. In the dungeon you will find many captives old and young, your brothers among them. Now that I have told you this are you going to spare my life? "

But the shepherd wrung the sparrow's neck for he knew that only in that way could the monster who had captured his brothers be killed.

Well, now that the dragon was dead the Tsar and all his courtiers came down from the hill and embraced the shepherd and told him what a brave youth he was.

"You have delivered us all from a horrid monster," the Tsar said, "and to show you my gratitude and the country's gratitude I offer you my daughter for wife."

"Thank you," said the shepherd, "but I couldn't think of marrying the Princess unless she is willing to marry me."

The Princess blushed and trembled just as she had blushed and trembled the night before and that morning, too, on the way to the lake. She tried to speak but could not at first. Then in a very little voice she said:

"As a Princess I think it is my duty to marry this brave shepherd who has delivered my country from this terrible dragon, and—and I think I should want to marry him anyway."

She said the last part of her speech in such a very low voice that only the shepherd himself heard it. But that was right enough because after all it was intended only for him.

So then and there beside the lake before even the shepherd had time to wash his face and hands and put on his smock the Tsar put the Princess's hand in his hand and pronounced them betrothed.

After that the shepherd bathed in the lake and then refreshed and clean he sounded his bagpipes and he and the Princess and the Tsar and all the courtiers returned to the city driving the sheep before them.

All the townspeople came out to meet them and they danced to the music of the bagpipes and there was great rejoicing both over the death of the dragon and over the betrothal of the Princess and the brave shepherd.

The wedding took place at once and the wedding festivities lasted a week. Such feasting as the townspeople had! Such music and dancing!

When the wedding festivities were ended, the shepherd told the Tsar who he really was.

" You say you're a Prince! " the Tsar cried, perfectly delighted at this news. Then he declared he wasn't in the least surprised. In fact, he said, he had suspected as much from the first!

" Do you think it likely," he asked somewhat pompously, " that any daughter of mine would fall in love with a man who wasn't a prince? "

" I think I'd have fallen in love with you whatever you were! " whispered the Princess to her young husband. But she didn't let her father hear her!

The Prince told the Tsar about his brothers' captivity and how he must go home to release them, and the

Tsar at once said that he and his bride might go provided they returned as soon as possible.

They agreed to this and the Tsar fitted out a splendid escort for them and sent them away with his blessing.

So the Prince now traveled back through the towns and villages of three kingdoms, across rivers and over mountains, no longer a humble shepherd on foot, but a rich and mighty personage riding in a manner that befitted his rank.

When he reached the deserted mill, his friend the old woman was waiting for him.

"I know, my Prince, you have succeeded for the monster has disappeared."

"Yes, granny, you are right: I have succeeded. I found the dragon in the lake, and the boar in the dragon, and the rabbit in the boar, and the pigeon in the rabbit, and the sparrow in the pigeon. I took the sparrow and killed it. So you are free now, granny, to return to your home. And soon all those other poor captives will be free."

He went behind the mill and found the three willow saplings. He cut them off and struck the old root. Sure enough a heavy iron door opened. This led down into a deep dungeon which was crowded with unfortunate prisoners. The Prince led them all out and sent them their various ways. He found his own two brothers among them and led them home to his father.

There was great rejoicing in the King's house, and in the King's heart, too, for he had given up hope of ever seeing any of his sons again.

The King was so charmed with the Princess that he said it was a pity that she couldn't marry his oldest son so that she might one day be Queen.

" The Youngest Prince is a capable young man," the King said, "and there's no denying that he managed this business of killing the dragon very neatly. But he is after all only the Youngest Prince with very little hope of succeeding to the kingdom. If you hadn't married him in such haste one of his older brothers might easily have fallen in love with you."

" I don't regret my haste," the Princess said. " Besides he is now my father's heir. But that doesn't matter for I should be happy with the Youngest Prince if he were only a shepherd."

THE LITTLE SINGING FROG

The Story of a Girl Whose Parents Were Ashamed of Her

THE LITTLE SINGING FROG

THERE was once a poor laborer and his wife who had no children. Every day the woman would sigh and say:

" If only we had a child! "

Then the man would sigh, too, and say:

" It would be pleasant to have a little daughter, wouldn't it? "

At last they went on a pilgrimage to a holy shrine and there they prayed God to give them a child.

" Any kind of a child! " the woman prayed. " I'd be thankful for a child of our own even if it were a frog! "

God heard their prayer and sent them a little daughter—not a little girl daughter, however, but a little frog daughter. They loved their little frog child dearly and played with her and laughed and clapped their hands as they watched her hopping about the house. But when the neighbors came in and whispered: " Why, that child of theirs is nothing but a frog! " they were ashamed and they decided that when people were about they had better keep their child hidden in a closet.

163

So the frog girl grew up without playmates of her own age, seeing only her father and mother. She used to play about her father as he worked. He was a vine-dresser in a big vineyard and of course it was great fun for the little frog girl to hop about among the vines.

Every day at noontime the woman used to come to the vineyard carrying her husband's dinner in a basket. The years went by and she grew old and feeble and the daily trip to the vineyard began to tire her and the basket seemed to her to grow heavier and heavier.

"Let me help you, mother," the frog daughter said. "Let me carry father's dinner to him and you sit home and rest."

So from that time on the frog girl instead of the old woman carried the dinner basket to the vineyard. While the old man ate, the frog girl would hop up into the branches of a tree and sing. She sang very sweetly and her old father, when he petted her, used to call her his Little Singing Frog.

Now one day while she was singing the Tsar's Young-est Son rode by and heard her. He stopped his horse and looked this way and that but for the life of him he couldn't see who it was who was singing so sweetly.

"Who is singing?" he asked the old man.

But the old man who, as I told you before, was

ashamed of his frog daughter before strangers, at first pretended not to hear and then, when the young Prince repeated his question, answered gruffly:

" There's no one singing! "

But the next day at the same hour when the Prince was again riding by he heard the same sweet voice and he stopped again and listened.

" Surely, old man," he said, " there is some one singing! It is a lovely girl, I know it is! Why, if I could find her, I'd be willing to marry her at once and take her home to my father, the Tsar! "

" Don't be rash, young man," the laborer said.

" I mean what I say! " the Prince declared. " I'd marry her in a minute! "

" Are you sure you would? "

" Yes, I'm sure! "

" Very well, then, we'll see."

The old man looked up into the tree and called:

" Come down, Little Singing Frog! A Prince wants to marry you! "

So the little frog girl hopped down from among the branches and stood before the Prince.

" She's my own daughter," the laborer said, " even if she does look like a frog."

" I don't care what she looks like," the Prince said.

"I love her singing and I love her. And I mean what I say: I'll marry her if she'll marry me. My father, the Tsar, bids me and my brothers present him our brides to-morrow. He bids all the brides bring him a flower and he says he'll give the kingdom to the prince whose bride brings the loveliest flower. Little Singing Frog, will you be my bride and will you come to Court to-morrow bringing a flower?"

"Yes, my Prince," the frog girl said, "I will. But I must not shame you by hopping to Court in the dust. I must ride. So, will you send me a snow-white cock from your father's barnyard?"

"I will," the Prince promised, and before night the snow-white cock had arrived at the laborer's cottage.

Early the next morning the frog girl prayed to the Sun.

"O golden Sun," she said, "I need your help! Give me some lovely clothes woven of your golden rays for I would not shame my Prince when I go to Court."

The Sun heard her prayer and gave her a gown of cloth of gold.

Instead of a flower she took a spear of wheat in her hand and then when the time came she mounted the white cock and rode to the palace.

This, the Bride of the Youngest Prince, Is My Choice

The guards at the palace gate at first refused to admit her.

"This is no place for frogs!" they said to her. "You're looking for a pond!"

But when she told them she was the Youngest Prince's bride, they were afraid to drive her away. So they let her ride through the gate.

"Strange!" they murmured to one another. "The Youngest Prince's bride! She looks like a frog and that was certainly a cock she was riding, wasn't it?"

They stepped inside the gates to look after her and then they saw an amazing sight. The frog girl, still seated on the white cock, was shaking out the folds of a golden gown. She dropped the gown over her head and instantly there was no frog and no white cock but a lovely maiden mounted on a snow-white horse!

Well, the frog girl entered the palace with two other girls, the promised brides of the older princes. They were just ordinary girls both of them. To see them you wouldn't have paid any attention to them one way or the other. But standing beside the lovely bride of the Youngest Prince they seemed more ordinary than ever.

The first girl had a rose in her hand. The Tsar looked at it and at her, sniffed his nose slightly, and turned his head.

The second girl had a carnation. The Tsar looked at her for a moment and murmured:

"Dear me, this will never do!"

Then he looked at the Youngest Prince's bride and his eye kindled and he said:

"Ah! This is something like!"

She gave him the spear of wheat and he took it and held it aloft. Then he reached out his other hand to her and had her stand beside him as he said to his sons and all the Court:

"This, the bride of the Youngest Prince, is my choice! See how beautiful she is! And yet she knows the useful as well as the beautiful for she has brought me a spear of wheat! The Youngest Prince shall be the Tsar after me and she shall be Tsarina!"

So the little frog girl of whom her parents were ashamed married the Youngest Prince and when the time came wore a Tsarina's crown.

THE NIGHTINGALE IN THE MOSQUE

*The Story of the Sultan's Youngest Son and the Princess
Flower o' the World*

THE NIGHTINGALE IN THE MOSQUE

THERE was once a Sultan who was so pious and devout that he spent many hours every day in prayer.

"For the glory of Allah," he thought to himself, "I ought to build the most beautiful mosque in the world."

So he called together the finest artisans in the country and told them what he wanted. He spent a third of his riches on the undertaking, and when the mosque was finished everybody said:

"See now, our Sultan has built the most beautiful mosque in the world for the greater glory of Allah!"

On the first day when the Sultan went to pray in the new mosque, a Dervish who was sitting cross-legged at the entrance spoke to him in a droning sing-song voice and said:

"Nay, but your mosque is not yet beautiful enough! There is something it lacks and your prayers will be unavailing!"

The words of the holy man grieved the Sultan and he had the mosque torn down and another built in its place even more beautiful.

"This is certainly the most beautiful mosque in the world!" the people said, and the Sultan's heart was very happy on the first day as he went in to pray.

But again the Dervish, seated at the entrance, said to him in his droning, sing-song voice:

"Nay, but your mosque is not yet beautiful enough! There is something it lacks and your prayers will be unavailing!"

At the holy man's words the Sultan had the second mosque torn down and a third one built, the most beautiful of them all. But when it was finished for a third time the Dervish droned out:

"Nay, but your mosque is not yet beautiful enough! There is something it lacks and your prayers will be unavailing!"

"What can I do?" the Sultan cried. "I have spent all my riches and now I have no means wherewith to build another mosque!"

He fell to grieving and nothing any one could say would comfort him.

His three sons came to him and said:

"Father, is there not something we can do for you?"

The Sultan sighed and shook his head.

"Nothing, my sons, unless indeed you were to find

8

8
8

out for me why my third mosque is not the most beautiful in the world."

"Brothers," the youngest suggested, "let us go to the Dervish and ask him why it is that the third mosque is not yet beautiful enough. Perhaps he will tell us what is lacking."

So they went to the Dervish and asked him what he meant by saying to the Sultan that the third mosque was not yet beautiful enough and they begged him to tell them what it was that was lacking.

The Dervish fixed his eyes in the distance and slightly swaying his body back and forth answered them in his sing-song tone.

"The mosque is beautiful," he said, "and the fountain in its midst is beautiful, but where is the glorious Nightingale Gisar? With the Nightingale Gisar singing beside the fountain, then indeed would the Sultan's third mosque be the most beautiful mosque in the world!"

"Only tell us where this glorious Nightingale is," the brothers begged, "and we will get him if it costs us our lives!"

"I cannot tell you that," the Dervish droned. "You will have to go out into the world and find him for yourselves."

So the three brothers returned to the Sultan and told him what the Dervish had said.

"All your third mosque lacks to be the most beautiful mosque in the world," they told him, "is the Nightingale Gisar singing beside the fountain. So grieve no more, father. We, your three sons, will go out into the world in quest of this glorious bird and within a year's time we will return with the bird in our hands if so be that it is anywhere to be found in all the wide world."

The Sultan blessed them and they set forth the three of them, side by side. They traveled together until they reached a place where three roads branched. Upon the stone of the left-hand road nothing was written. Upon the stone of the middle road was the inscription: *Who goes this way returns.* The inscription on the third stone read: *Who goes this way shall meet many dangers and may never return.*

"Let us part here," the oldest brother said, "and each take a separate road. Then if all goes well, let us meet here again on this same spot one year hence. As our father's oldest son it would be wrong for me to run unnecessary risks, so I will take the left-hand road."

"And I will take the middle road," the second brother cried.

The Youngest Brother laughed and said:

"That leaves the dangerous road for me! Very well, brothers, that's the very road I wish to take for why should I leave home if it were not to have adventures! Farewell then until we meet again in one year's time."

The oldest traveled his safe road until he reached a city where he became a barber. He asked every man whose head he shaved:

"Do you know anything of the Nightingale Gisar?"

He never found any one who had even heard of the bird, so after a time he stopped asking.

The second brother followed the middle road to a city where he settled down and opened a coffee-house.

"Have you ever heard of a glorious Nightingale known as Gisar?" he asked at first of every traveler who came in and sipped his coffee. Not one of them ever had and as time went by the second brother gradually stopped even making inquiries.

The Youngest Brother who took the dangerous road came to no city at all but to a far-off desolate place without houses or highways or farms. Wild creatures hid in the brush and snakes glided in and out among the rocks. One day he came upon a wild woman who was combing her hair with a branch of juniper.

"That isn't the way to comb your hair," the Youngest Brother said. "Here, let me show you."

He took his own comb and smoothed out all the tangles in the wild woman's hair until she was comfortable and happy.

" You have been very kind to me," she said. " Now isn't there something I can do for you in return? "

" I am looking for the Nightingale Gisar. If you know where that glorious bird is, tell me and that will more than repay me."

But the wild woman had never heard of the Nightingale Gisar.

" Only wild animals inhabit this desolate place," she said, " and a few wild people like me. The Nightingale Gisar is not here."

" Then I must go farther," the Youngest Brother said.

This the wild woman begged him not to do.

" Beyond these mountains," she said, " is a wilder desert with fiercer animals. Turn back while you can."

" No," the Youngest Brother insisted, " I'm going as God leads me."

So he left the wild woman and crossed the mountains. He went on and on until he was footsore and weary. Then at last he came to the Tiger's house.

The Tiger's wife met him.

" Be off, young man! " she warned him, " or the Tiger when he comes home will eat you! "

" No! " said the Youngest Brother, " now I'm here I'm going to stay for I have a question to ask the Tiger."

The Tiger's wife was making bread. When the dough was ready to go into the oven, she leaned over the glowing embers of the fire and began to brush them aside with her body.

" Stop! " the Youngest Brother cried. " You will burn yourself! "

" But how else can I brush aside the glowing embers? " the Tiger's wife asked.

" I'll show you."

The Youngest Brother cut a branch from a tree outside and fashioned it into a rough broom. Then he showed the Tiger's wife how to use it.

" Ah! " she said gratefully, " before this always when I've baked bread I've been sick for ten days afterwards. Now I shall be sick no more for you have taught me how to use a broom. In return let me hide you in a dark corner and when the Tiger comes home I'll tell him how kind you have been and perhaps he will not eat you."

So she hid the Youngest Brother in a dark corner

and when the Tiger came home she met him and
said:

"See, I have baked bread to-day but I am not sick,
for a youth has shown me how I can brush aside the
embers without burning myself."

The Tiger was overjoyed to hear that his wife had
been able to bake bread without being made sick and he
swore to be a brother to him who had taught her the use
of a broom. So the Youngest Brother came out from
the dark corner where he was hiding and the Tiger made
him welcome.

"What are you doing wandering about in this wild
country?" the Tiger asked.

"I am searching for the Nightingale Gisar and I have
come to you to ask you if you can tell me where I can
find that glorious bird."

The Tiger had never heard of the Nightingale Gisar
but he thought that his oldest brother the Lion might
know.

"Go straight on from here," he said, "until you come
to the Lion's house. His old wife stands outside facing
the house with her long thin old dugs thrown over her
shoulders. Go up to her from behind and take her dugs
and put them in your mouth and suck them and when
she asks you who you are, say: 'Don't you know me,

old mother? I'm your oldest cub.' Then she will lead you in to the Lion who is so old that his eyelids droop. Prop them open and when he sees you he will tell you what he knows."

So the Youngest Brother went on to the Lion's house and he found the Lion's old wife standing outside as the Tiger said he would. He did all the Tiger had told him to do and when the Lion's wife asked him who he was, he said: 'Don't you know me, old mother? I'm your oldest cub.' Then the Lion's old wife led him in to the Lion and he propped open the Lion's drooping eyelids and asked about the Nightingale Gisar.

The old Lion shook his head.

" I have never heard of the Nightingale Gisar. He has never sung in this wild place. Turn back, young man, and seek him elsewhere. Beyond this is a country of wilder creatures where you will only lose your life."

" That is as God wills," the Youngest Brother said.

With that he bade the old Lion and his old wife farewell and pushed on into the farther wilds. The mountains grew more and more rugged, the plains more parched and barren, and the Youngest Son was hard put to it to find food from day to day.

Once when he was crossing a desert three eagles

swooped down upon him and it was all he could do to fight them off. He slashed at them with his sword and succeeded in cutting off the beak of one, a wing of another, and a leg of the third. He put these three things in his bag as trophies.

He came at last to a hut where an old woman was baking cakes on the hearth.

"God bless you, granny!" he said. "Can you give me a bite of supper and shelter for the night?"

The old woman shook her head.

"My boy, you had better not stop here. I have three daughters and if they were to come home and find you here, they'd kill you."

But the Youngest Brother insisted that he was not afraid and at last the old woman let him stay. She hid him in the corner behind the firewood and warned him to keep still.

Presently the three eagles whom he had maimed came flying into the hut. The old woman put a bowl of milk on the table, the birds dipped in the milk, and lo! their feather shirts opened and they stepped out three maidens. One of them had lost her lips, one an arm, and the third a leg.

"Ah!" they cried to their mother, "see what has befallen us! If only the youth who maimed us would return the beak and the wing and the leg that he hacked off, we would tell him anything he wants to know."

At that the Youngest Brother stepped out from behind the firewood and said:

"Tell me then where I can find the Nightingale Gisar and you shall have back your beak and your wing and your leg."

He opened his bag and the maidens were overjoyed to see their beak and their wing and their leg. Then they told the Youngest Brother all they knew about the Nightingale Gisar.

"Far from here," they said, "there is a Warrior Princess, so beautiful that men call her Flower o' the World. She has the Nightingale Gisar in a golden cage hanging in her own chamber. The chamber door is guarded by a lion and a wolf and a tiger for the Flower 'o' the World knows that she will have to marry the man who steals from her the Nightingale Gisar."

"How can a man enter the chamber of the Flower o' the World?" the Youngest Brother asked.

"For a few moments at midnight," the sisters told him, "the three animals sleep. During those few moments a man could enter the chamber, get the Nightingale Gisar, and escape. But even then he might not be safe for the Flower o' the World might gather her army together and pursue him."

"Now tell me how to reach the palace of that Warrior Princess, Flower o' the World."

"You could never get there alone," they told him, "the way is too long and the dangers are too many. Stay here with us for three months and at the end of three months we will carry you thither on our wings."

So for three months the Youngest Brother stayed on in the hut with the old woman and her three daughters. The three daughters flew in their eagle shirts to the spring of the Water of Life and bathing in that magic pool they made grow on again the beak and the wing and the leg which the Youngest Brother had hacked off.

At the end of three months they carried the Youngest Brother on their wings to the distant kingdom where the Warrior Princess, Flower o' the World, lived.

At midnight they set him down in front of the palace and he slipped unseen through the guards at the gate and through the halls of the palace to the Princess's own chamber. The lion, the wolf, and the tiger were asleep and he was able to push back the curtain before which they were lying and creep up to the Princess's very bedside without being discovered.

He looked once at the sleeping Flower o' the World and she was so beautiful that he dared not look again for fear he should forget the Nightingale Gisar and betray himself by crying out.

At the head of the bed were four lighted candles and at the foot four unlighted ones. He blew out the lighted ones and lit the others. Then quickly he took the golden cage in which the Nightingale Gisar was perched asleep, unfastened it from the golden chain on which it was hanging, and hurried out. The eagles were waiting for him and at once they spread their wings and carried him away.

They put him down at the crossroads where he had parted from his brothers just one year before. Then they bade him farewell and flew off to their home in the desert.

"My brothers will probably be here in an hour or so," the Youngest Son thought. "I had better wait for them."

He felt sleepy, so he lay down by the roadside and closed his eyes.

While he slept his brothers arrived and of course the first thing they saw was the golden cage and the Nightingale Gisar.

Then envy and hatred filled their hearts and they

began cursing and complaining to think that he who was the Youngest had succeeded where they had failed.

" We'll be the laughing-stock of the whole country! " they said, " if we let him come home carrying the Nightingale Gisar! Let us take the bird while he sleeps and hurry home with it. Then if he comes home later and says it was he who really found the bird no one will believe him."

So they beat their brother into insensibility and tore his clothes to rags to make him think that he had been set upon by robbers, and then taking the golden cage and the Nightingale Gisar they hurried home and presented themselves to their father, the Sultan.

" Here, O father," they said, " is the Nightingale Gisar! To get this glorious bird for you we have endured all the perils in the world! "

" And your Youngest Brother," the Sultan asked, " where is he? "

" The Youngest? Think no more of him, father, for he is unworthy to be your son. Instead of searching the wide world for the Nightingale Gisar, he settled down in the first city he reached and lived a life of idleness and ease. Some say he became a barber and some say he opened a coffee-house and spent his days chatting with passing travelers. He has not come home with us for no doubt it shames him to know that we have succeeded where he has failed."

The Sultan was grieved to hear this evil report of his Youngest Son, but he was overjoyed to have the Nightingale Gisar. He had the golden cage carried to the mosque and hung beside the fountain in the court.

But imagine his disappointment when the bird refused to sing!

"Let him who found the Nightingale come to the mosque," the Dervish said in his droning sing-song voice, "and then the Nightingale will sing."

The Sultan immediately sent for his two sons. They came but still the bird was silent.

"See now," the Sultan said, "my two sons are here and yet the bird is silent."

But the Dervish would only repeat:

"Let him who found the Nightingale come to the mosque and then the Nightingale will sing."

The next day a youth in rags whom nobody knew entered the mosque to pray and instantly the Nightingale began to sing.

A messenger was sent running to the Sultan with the news that the Nightingale was singing. The Sultan hurried to the mosque but by the time he got there the beggar youth was gone and the Nightingale had stopped singing.

"Now that I'm here," cried the Sultan, "why does the bird not sing?"

The Dervish, swaying his body gently back and forth, made answer as before:

"Let him who found the Nightingale come to the mosque and then the Nightingale will sing."

Thereafter every day when the beggar youth came to the mosque to pray the Nightingale sang, and always when the Sultan approached the beggar walked away and the bird stopped singing. At last people began whispering:

"Strange that the Nightingale should sing only when that beggar youth is near! And yet the Dervish says it will not sing unless he who found it comes to the mosque! What can he mean?"

Report of the beggar youth reached the ears of the Sultan and he went to the Dervish and questioned him.

"Why do you say that the Nightingale Gisar will not sing unless he who found him comes to the mosque? Lo, here are my two sons who found him and the bird remains silent, yet people tell me that when a certain beggar comes to the mosque he sings. Why does he not sing when I and my two sons come to pray?"

And always the Dervish made the same answer in the same sing-song voice:

"Let him who found the Nightingale come to the mosque and then the Nightingale will sing."

Soon a terrifying rumor spread through the land that a great Warrior Princess called Flower o' the World was coming with a mighty army to make war on the Sultan and to destroy his city. Her army far outnumbered the Sultan's and when she encamped in a broad valley over against the city the Sultan's people, seeing her mighty hosts, were filled with dread and besought their ruler to make peace with the Princess at any cost. So the Sultan called his heralds and sent them to her and through them he said:

"Demand of me what you will even to my life but spare my city."

The Warrior Princess returned this answer:

"I will spare you and your city provided you deliver me your son who stole from me the Nightingale Gisar. Him I shall have executed or let live as it pleases me."

Now the Sultan's two sons knew that the Flower o' the World was fated to marry the man who had stolen from her the Nightingale Gisar, so when they heard the Princess's demand they were overjoyed thinking that she would have to fall in love with one of them. So they disputed at great length as to which of them had done the actual deed of taking the bird, each insisting that it was he and not his brother. The Sultan himself had finally to decide between them.

"You have told me," he said, "that you captured the bird together. As that is the case and as I can't send you both to the Warrior Princess it is only right that the older should go."

So under a splendid escort the oldest son rode to the tent of the Warrior Princess. She bade him enter alone and when he appeared before her she looked at him long and steadily. Then she said:

"Nay, but you are never the man who stole from me the Nightingale Gisar! You would lack the courage to face the perils of the way!"

The oldest prince answered the Flower o' the World craftily:

"But how, Princess, if I did not steal from you the Nightingale Gisar was I then able to bring back that glorious bird and hang his cage beside the fountain in the mosque?"

But Flower o' the World was not to be deceived by such specious words.

"Tell me then," she said, "if it was you who stole

my glorious Nightingale, where did you find him hanging in his golden cage? "

The oldest prince could not answer this, so he said at random:

" I found his golden cage hanging in the cypress tree that grows in the garden of your palace."

" Enough! " cried the Princess.

She clapped her hands and when her guards appeared she said to them:

" Have this man executed at once and let his head be sent to the Sultan with the message: *This is the head of a liar and a coward! Send me at once your son who stole my glorious Nightingale Gisar or I will march against your city!* "

The Sultan was greatly shocked to receive this message together with the head of his oldest son.

" Alas! " he cried, calling his second son, " would that I had listened to you when you insisted that it was you and not your brother who actually did the deed! Unhappily I listened to your brother! See now the awful result of this mistake! Go you now to this heartless Princess whom men call Flower o' the World or else our poor defenseless city will have to pay the penalty."

So the second prince was taken to the tent of the Warrior Maiden and she put to him the same questions and he fared even worse than his brother had fared. So his head, too, was sent to the Sultan with this message:

" *Send me no more liars and cowards but the son who actually did steal from me my glorious Nightingale Gisar.*"

In despair the Sultan went to the mosque to pray. As he bowed his head he heard the Nightingale burst forth in song. Then when he looked up he saw a beggar youth standing near the fountain.

When his prayers were finished the Sultan went outside to the Dervish and said to him:

" The Warrior Princess, Flower o' the World, demands that I send her another son. I know not where my Third Son is. What shall I do?"

Without looking at the Sultan the Dervish answered in his sing-song voice:

" Send her the son for whom the Nightingale sings."

The Sultan turned away in disappointment, not understanding what the Dervish meant, but one of his attendants plucked his sleeve and whispered:

" The Nightingale sings for yonder beggar youth. Perhaps it is he the Dervish means. Why not ask him if he will go to Flower o' the World in place of your Youngest Son?"

The Flower o' the World Asleep

The Sultan nodded, so the attendant called the beggar youth and the Sultan asked him would he go to the Warrior Princess as the Youngest Prince.

"Allah alone knows where my Youngest Son is," the Sultan said, "but he is just about your age and if you were washed and anointed and dressed in fitting garments you would not be unlike him."

The beggar youth said he would go but he insisted on going just as he was. The Sultan begged him to go dressed as a prince or the Flower o' the World might not receive him.

"No," said the youth, "I shall go as a beggar or not at all. It is for the Flower o' the World to know me whether or not I am the Sultan's Youngest Son and the man who stole from her the Nightingale Gisar."

So he went as he was to the tent of the Flower o' the World and her warriors when they saw him coming said to the Princess:

"This Sultan mocks you and sends you a beggar when you demand his Third Son."

But the Flower o' the World ordered them all out and bade the beggar enter alone. She looked at him long and steadily and she saw through his rags that he was indeed a noble youth with a body made strong and beautiful through exercise and toil and she thought to herself:

" It were not a hard fate to marry this youth! "

Then she questioned him:

" Are you the Sultan's Third Son? "

" I am."

" Then why are you dressed as a beggar? "

" Because I was set upon at the crossroads and beaten insensible and my clothes torn to rags. I was coming home with the Nightingale Gisar in my hands and I lay down at the roadside to rest while I awaited the coming of my brothers. When I awoke to consciousness the Nightingale and its golden cage were gone. I came home to my father's city as a beggar and there they told me that my brothers had come just before me bringing with them the Nightingale and boasting of the perils they had been through and the dangers they had faced. But the Nightingale, they told me, hanging in its golden cage beside the fountain, was silent. Yet when I went to the mosque it always sang."

The Warrior Princess looked deep into his eyes and knew that he was speaking truth. Her heart was touched with compassion at the wrong he had suffered from his brothers, but she hid her feelings and questioned him further.

" Then it was you," she said, " who really took from me my glorious Nightingale Gisar? "

" Yes, Princess, it was. I crept past the lion and the wolf and the tiger just after midnight while they slept. I blew out the four candles at the head of your bed and lighted those at the foot. The golden cage of the Nightingale was hanging from a golden chain. Before I unfastened it I looked at you once, as you lay sleeping, and dared not look a second time."

" Why not? " the Princess asked.

" Because, O Flower o' the World, you were so beautiful that I feared, were I to look again, I should forget the Nightingale Gisar and cry out in ecstacy."

Then the compassion in the Princess's heart changed to love and she knew for a certainty that this was the man she was fated to wed.

She clapped her hands and when the guards came in she said to them:

" Call my warriors together that I may show them the Sultan's Youngest Son and the man who stole from me my glorious Nightingale Gisar and whom I am fated to wed."

So the warriors came in until they crowded the tent

to its utmost. Then the Princess stood up and took
the Sultan's Youngest Son by the hand and presented
him to the warriors and told them of his great bravery
and courage and of all the perils he had endured in
order to get the Nightingale Gisar for his father's
mosque.

"He came to me now as a beggar," she said, "but I
knew him at once for truth was in his mouth and courage in his eye. Behold, O warriors, your future lord!"

Then the warriors waved their swords and cried:

"Long live the Flower o' the World! Long live the
Sultan's Youngest Son!"

All the Princess's army when they heard the news
raised such a mighty shout that the people in the Sultan's city heard and were filled with dread not knowing
what it meant. But soon they knew and then they, too,
went mad with joy that what had threatened to be a
war was turning to a wedding!

The Flower o' the World and her chief warriors and
with them the Youngest Prince rode slowly to the city.
The Prince was now dressed as befitted his rank and
the Sultan when he saw him recognized him at once.

"Allah be praised!" he cried, "my Youngest Son
lives!"

Then they told him all—how it was this Prince and

not the older brothers who had found the Nightingale Gisar and how the older brothers had robbed him of his prize and beaten him insensible.

When the Sultan heard how wicked his older sons had been his grief for their death was assuaged.

" Allah be praised," he said, " that I have at least one son who is worthy! "

After the betrothal ·ceremony the Sultan and the Youngest Prince went to the mosque to pray. While they prayed the Nightingale sang so gloriously that it seemed to them they were no longer on earth but in Paradise.

When their prayers were finished and they were passing out, the Dervish raised his sing-song voice and said:

" Now indeed is the Sultan's Mosque the most beautiful Mosque in the World for the Nightingale Gisar sings beside the Fountain! "

THE GIRL IN THE CHEST

The Story of the Third Sister Who Was Brave and Good

THE GIRL IN THE CHEST

THERE was once a horrible Vampire who took the form of a handsome young man and went to the house of an old woman who had three daughters and pretended he wanted to marry the oldest.

"I live far from here," the Vampire said. "I own my own farm and am well-to-do and in marrying me your daughter would get a desirable husband. Indeed, I am so well off that I don't have to ask any dowry."

Now the old woman was so poor that she couldn't have given a penny of dowry. That was the only reason why all three of her daughters hadn't long ago been married to youths of their own village. So when the stranger said he would require no dowry, the old woman whispered to her oldest daughter:

"He seems to be all right. Perhaps you had better take him."

The poor girl accepted her mother's advice and that afternoon started off with the Vampire who said he would lead her home and marry her.

They walked a great distance and as evening came

on they reached a wild ghostly spot which frightened the girl half to death.

"This way, my dear," the Vampire said, pushing her into an opening in the earth. "We take this underground passage and soon we'll be home."

The passage led to a sort of cave which really was the Vampire's home.

"What an awful place!" the poor girl cried in terror. "Let me out!"

"Let you out, indeed!" the Vampire sneered, taking his own horrible shape and laughing cruelly. "Here you are and here you stay and if you don't do everything I tell you, I'll soon finish you! Here now, drink this."

He offered the poor girl a pitcher and when she saw what was in it she nearly fainted with horror.

"No!" she cried. "I won't! I won't!"

"If you don't drink this," the Vampire said, darkly, "then I'll drink you!"

And with that he killed her with no more feeling than if she were a fly.

Then in a short time he went back to the old woman and said:

"Dear mother, my poor wife is ill and she begs that you send her your second daughter to nurse her. She asks for her sister night and day and I fear she will die unless she sees her."

When the poor old mother heard this, she begged the second daughter to go at once with the young man and nurse her sick sister.

Well, the same thing happened to the second sister and in no time at all the Vampire had killed her, too, to satisfy his awful thirst.

Then he returned again to the old mother and this time he pretended that both sisters were sick and were crying for the third sister to come and nurse them. So the poor old woman sent her Youngest Daughter away with the Vampire.

The Youngest Sister when she found out the truth about the horrid Vampire didn't sit down and weep helplessly as the others had done and wait for the Vampire to kill her, but she prayed God's help and then tried to find some way of escape.

There were doors in the cave which the Vampire told her were doors to closets she must not enter. When the Vampire was out she opened these doors and found that they all led into long underground passages.

"This is my one chance to get back to earth!" the girl thought and commending her undertaking to God she fled down one of the passages.

You may be sure the Vampire when he came back and found her gone fell into a great rage. He went running wildly up and down the various passages and lost so much time searching the wrong passages that the girl was able to make good her escape and reach the upper world in safety.

She came out in a wood with no sign of human habitation anywhere in sight.

"What shall I do now?" she thought. "If I stay here alone and unprotected some wild beast or evil creature may get me."

So she knelt down and prayed God to give her a chest that she could lock from the inside with one of her own golden hairs so securely that no one could force it open. God heard her prayer and presently behind some bushes she found just such a chest. When it grew dark and she was ready to go to bed, she crept into the chest, locked it with a hair, and slept peacefully knowing that nothing could harm her.

So she lived in the wood some time, eating berries and fruits, and sleeping safely in the chest.

Now it so happened that the King's son one morning went hunting in this very wood and caught a glimpse of the girl as she was gathering berries. He thought he had never seen such a beautiful creature and in-

stantly he fell in love with her. But when he reached
the clump of bushes where he had seen her, she was
gone. He called his huntsmen together and told them
to search everywhere. They hunted for hours and all
they could find was a chest. They tried to open the
chest to see what was in it but couldn't.

"Waste no more time over it," the Prince said at
last. "Carry it home to the palace as it is and have
it placed in my chamber."

The huntsmen did this and a few hours later when
the girl peeped out of her chest she found herself alone
in the Prince's chamber. His supper was standing on
a table in readiness for his coming. The girl ate the
supper and was safely back in her chest before he arrived. When he did come the Prince was amazed to
see empty plates and called the servants to know who
had eaten his supper. The servants were as much surprised as the Prince and declared that no one had entered the chamber.

The same thing happened the next day and the following day the Prince had one of his servants hide behind the curtains and watch to find out if possible how
the food disappeared.

The story the servant had to tell of what he saw
was so thrilling that the Prince could scarcely wait

for the next day when he himself hid behind the curtains and watched.

The serving people put the food on the table and retired and presently the lid of the chest opened and the Prince saw the beautiful maiden of the wood step out. When she sat down at the table the Prince slipped up behind her and caught her in his arms.

"You lovely creature!" he said, "I'm not going to let you escape me again!"

At first the girl was greatly frightened but the Prince reassured her, telling her that he loved her dearly and only wanted to make her his wife.

He led her at once to the King, his father, and the girl was so modest and lovely that the King soon agreed to the marriage.

Everybody in court was delighted—everybody, that is, but the Chamberlain who had had hopes of marrying his own daughter to the Prince. His daughter was an ugly ill-tempered girl and the Prince had never once even looked at her. The Chamberlain was sure, however, that with a little more time he could arrange the match to his liking. So the appearance of this beautiful girl who came from Heaven knows where threw him into a fearful rage and he decided to do away with her at any cost. Now he had in his employ a great burly

The Chest Opened and the Prince Saw the Beautiful Maiden

Blackamoor. He called this fellow to him and he told him that he must kidnap the girl at once and kill her. The Blackamoor who was accustomed to do such deeds for the Chamberlain nodded and said he would.

So when the palace was quiet that night he stole to the bedchamber where the girl was lying asleep, threw a great robe over her head to stifle her cries, and carried her off. She fainted away from fright and the Blackamoor thinking her dead tossed her into a field of nettles in the outskirts of the town.

Now, as you can imagine, in the morning there was a great uproar in the palace when it was discovered that the Prince's beautiful bride-to-be had disappeared. The Prince was utterly grief-stricken and refused to eat. The King and all the ladies of the court tried their best to comfort him but he turned away from them declaring he would die if his bride were not restored to him.

The rascally Chamberlain put his handkerchief to his eyes and pretended to weep he was so affected by the sight of the Prince's grief.

" My dear boy," he said, " I would that I could find this maiden for you! It breaks my heart to see you sad and unhappy! But I'm sorry to tell you that I fear she was a Vila and not a human maiden at all.

You know how mysteriously she came, and now she's gone just as mysteriously. So put the thought of her out of your mind and I'm sure you'll soon find a human maiden who is worthy of your love. Come here, my daughter, and tell the Prince how sorry you are that he is in grief."

But the sight of the Chamberlain's ugly daughter only made the Prince long the more for the beautiful girl who was gone.

She meantime had found refuge in the hut of an old woman who had heard her groan in the early dawn when she lay among the nettles and had taken compassion on her.

"You may stay with me until you're well," the old woman said.

The girl was young and healthy and in a day or two had recovered the ill treatment she had suffered at the hands of the Blackamoor.

"Won't you let me live with you awhile, granny?" she said to the old woman. "I'll cook and scrub and work and you won't have to regret the little I eat."

"Can you cook? Because if you can perhaps you know a dish that would tempt the appetite of our poor young Prince," the old woman said. "You know the poor boy has had a terrible disappointment in love and he refuses to eat. The heralds were out this morning proclaiming that the King would richly reward any one who could prepare a dish that would tempt the Prince's appetite."

"Granny!" the girl said, "I know a wonderful way to prepare beans! Let me cook a dish of beans and do you carry them to the palace."

So the girl cooked the beans and placed them prettily in a dish and on one side of the dish she put a tiny little ringlet of her own golden hair.

"If he sees the hair," she thought to herself, "he'll know the beans are from me."

And that's exactly what happened. To please his father the Prince had consented to look at every dish as it came. He had already looked at hundreds of them before the old woman arrived and turned away from them all. Then the old woman came. As she passed before the Prince, she lifted the cover of the dish, held it towards him, and curtsied. The Prince was just about to turn away when he saw the tiny ringlet of hair.

"Oh!" he said. "Wait a minute! Those beans look good!"

To the King's delight he took the dish out of the old woman's hand, examined it carefully, and when no one was looking slipped the ringlet into his pocket. Then he ate the beans—every last one of them!

The King gave the old woman some golden ducats and begged her to prepare another dish for the Prince on the morrow.

So the next day the girl again sent a tiny ringlet of her hair on the side of the plate and again the Prince after scorning all the other food offered him took the old woman's dish and ate it clean.

On the third day the Prince engaged the old woman in conversation.

" Where do you live, granny? "

" In a little tumble-down house beside the nettles," she told him.

" Do you live alone? "

" Just now," the old woman said, " I have a dear girl living with me. I found her one morning lying in the nettles where some ruffians had left her for dead. She's a good girl and she scrubs and bakes and cooks for me and lets me rest my poor old bones."

Now the Prince knew what he wanted to know.

" Granny," he said, " to-morrow's Sunday. Now I want you to stay home in the afternoon because I'm coming to see you."

In great excitement the old woman hurried home

and told the girl that the Prince was coming to see
on Sunday afternoon.

"He mustn't see me!" the girl said. "I'll hide in
the bread trough under a cloth and if he goes looking
for me you tell him that I've gone out."

"Foolish child!" the old woman said. "Why should
you hide from a handsome young man like the Prince?"

But the girl insisted and at last when Sunday afternoon came the old woman was forced to let her lie down
in the bread trough and cover her with a cloth.

The Prince arrived and when he found the old woman
there alone he was mightily disappointed.

"Where's that girl who lives with you?" he asked.

"She's gone out," the old woman said.

"Then I think I'll wait till she comes back."

This made the old woman feel nervous.

"But, my Prince, I don't know when she's coming
back."

Just then the Prince thought he saw something move
in the bread trough.

"What's that lumpy thing in the bread trough,
granny?"

"That? Oh, that's just dough that's rising, my
Prince. I'm baking to-day."

"Then make me a loaf, granny. I'll wait for it

until it rises and until you bake it. Then I'll eat it hot out of the oven."

What was the old woman to say to that? She fussed and fidgeted and thought again what a foolish young girl that was to be hiding in the bread trough when there was a handsome young Prince in the room.

" I don't know why that dough doesn't rise," she remarked at last.

" Perhaps there's something the matter with it," the Prince said.

Before the old woman could stop him, he jumped up, tossed the cloth aside, and there was his lovely bride!

" Why are you hiding from me? " he asked as he lifted her up and kissed her tenderly.

" Because I knew if you really loved me you would find me," she said.

" Now that I have found you," the Prince declared, " I shall never let you leave me again."

Then the girl told the Prince about the wicked Chamberlain and the Blackamoor and it was all she and the old woman could do to keep the Prince from drawing his sword and rushing out instantly to kill both of them.

The old woman begged the Prince to take the girl secretly to the King and have the King hear her story, and then let him pass judgment on the Chamberlain according to the laws of the land. At last the Prince agreed to this.

So they covered the girl's head with a veil and took her to the King. When the King heard her story he called the court together at once and told them the outrage that had been committed against his son's promised bride. He commanded that the murderous Blackamoor be executed the next day and he decreed that the Chamberlain and his wicked daughter be stripped of their lands and riches and sent into exile.

Let us hope that exile taught them the evil of their ways and made them repent.

As for the girl, she married the Prince and they lived together in great happiness. And she deserved to be happy, too, for she was a brave birl and a good girl and God loves people who are brave and good and blesses them.

THE WONDERFUL HAIR

The Story of a Poor Man Who Dreamed of an Angel

THE WONDERFUL HAIR

THERE was once a poor man who had so many children that he was at his wit's end how to feed them all and clothe them.

"Unless something turns up soon," he thought to himself, "we shall all starve to death. Poor youngsters—I'm almost tempted to kill them with my own hands to save them from suffering the pangs of hunger!"

That night before he went to sleep he prayed God to give him help. God heard his prayer and sent an angel to him in a dream.

The angel said to him:

"To-morrow morning when you wake, put your hand under your pillow and you will find a mirror, a red handkerchief, and an embroidered scarf. Without saying a word to any one hide these things in your shirt and go out to the woods that lie beyond the third hill from the village. There you will find a brook. Follow it until you come to a beautiful maiden who is bathing in its waters. You will know her from the great masses of golden hair that fall down over her shoulders. She

will speak to you but do you be careful not to answer.
If you say a word to her she will be able to bewitch
you. She will hold out a comb to you and ask you to
comb her hair. Take the comb and do as she asks. Then
part her back hair carefully and you will see one hair
that is coarser than the others and as red as blood.
Wrap this firmly around one of your fingers and jerk
it out. Then flee as fast as you can. She will pursue
you and each time as she is about to overtake you drop
first the embroidered scarf, then the red handkerchief,
and last the mirror. If you reach the hill nearest your
own village you are safe for she can pursue you no
farther. Take good care of the single hair for it is of
great value and you can sell it for many golden ducats."

In the morning when the poor man awoke and put
his hand under his pillow he found the mirror and the
handkerchief and the scarf just as the angel had said
he would. So he hid them carefully in his shirt and
without telling any one where he was going he went
to the woods beyond the third hill from the village.
Here he found the brook and followed it until he came
to a pool where he saw a lovely maiden bathing.

" Good day to you! " she said politely.

The poor man remembering the angel's warning made
no answer.

The Mirror, the Handkerchief, and the Embroidered Scarf

The maiden held out a golden comb.

" Please comb my hair for me, won't you? "

The man nodded and took the comb. Then he parted the long tresses behind and and searched here and there and everywhere until he found the one hair that was blood-red in color and coarser than the others. He twisted this firmly around his finger, jerked it quickly out, and fled.

" Oh! " cried the maiden. " What are you doing? Give me back my one red hair! "

She jumped to her feet and ran swiftly after him. As she came close to him, he dropped behind him the embroidered scarf. She stooped and picked it up and examined it awhile. Then she saw the man was escaping, so she tossed the scarf aside and again ran after him. This time he dropped the red handkerchief. Its bright color caught the maiden's eye and she picked it up and lost a few more minutes admiring it while the man raced on. Then the maiden remembered him, threw away the handkerchief, and started off again in pursuit.

This time the man dropped the mirror and the maiden who of course was a Vila and had never seen a mirror before picked it up and looked at it and when she saw the lovely reflection of herself she was so amazed that she kept on looking and looking. She was still

looking in it and still admiring her own beauty when
the man reached the third hill beyond which the maiden
couldn't follow him.

So the poor man got home with the hair safely wound
about his finger.

"It must be of great value," he thought to himself.
"I'll take it to the city and offer it for sale there."

So the next day he went to the city and went about
offering his wonderful hair to the merchants.

"What's so wonderful about it?" they asked him.

"I don't know, but I do know it's of great value,"
he told them.

"Well," said one of them, "I'll give you one golden
ducat for it."

He was a shrewd buyer and the others hearing his
bid of one golden ducat decided that he must know
that the hair was of much greater value. So they began
to outbid him until the price offered the poor man
reached one hundred golden ducats. But the poor man
insisted that this was not enough.

"One hundred golden ducats not enough for one
red hair!" cried the merchants.

They pretended to be disgusted that any one would
refuse such a price for one red hair, but in reality they
were all firmly convinced by this time that it was a

magic hair and probably worth any amount of money in the world.

The whole city became excited over the wonderful hair for which all the merchants were bidding and for a time nothing else was talked about. The matter was reported to the Tsar and at once he said that he himself would buy the hair for one thousand golden ducats.

One thousand golden ducats! After that there was no danger of the poor man's many children dying of starvation.

And what do you suppose the Tsar did with the hair? He had it split open very carefully and inside he found a scroll of great importance to mankind for on it were written many wonderful secrets of nature.

THE BEST WISH

The Story of Three Brothers and an Angel

THE BEST WISH

THERE were once three brothers whose only possession was a pear tree. They took turns guarding it. That is to say while two of them went to work the third stayed at home to see that no harm came to the pear tree.

Now it happened that an Angel from heaven was sent down to test the hearts of the three brothers. The Angel took the form of a beggar and approaching the pear tree on a day when the oldest brother was guarding it, he held out his hand and said:

"In heaven's name, brother, give me a ripe pear."

The oldest brother at once handed him a pear, saying:

"This one I can give you because it is mine, but none of the others because they belong to my brothers."

The Angel thanked him and departed.

The next day when the second brother was on guard he returned in the same guise and again begged the charity of a ripe pear.

"Take this one," the second brother said. "It is

231

mine and I can give it away. I can't give away any
of the others because they belong to my brothers."

The Angel thanked the second brother and departed.

The third day he had exactly the same experience
with the youngest brother.

On the following day the Angel, in the guise of a
monk, came to the brothers' house very early while they
were still all at home.

" My sons," he said, " come with me and perhaps I
can find you something better to do than guard a single
pear tree."

The brothers agreed and they all started out together. After walking some time they came to the
banks of a broad deep river.

" My son," the Angel said, addressing the oldest
brother, " if I were to grant you one wish, what would
you ask? "

" I'd be happy," the oldest brother said, " if all this
water was turned into wine and belonged to me."

The Angel lifted his staff and made the sign of the
cross and lo! the water became wine from great wine-
presses. At once numbers of casks appeared and men
filling them and rolling them about. A huge industry
sprang up with sheds and storehouses and wagons and

The Angel Took the Form of a Beggar

men running hither and thither and addressing the oldest brother respectfully as "Master!"

"You have your wish," the Angel said. "See that you do not forget God's poor now that you are rich. Farewell."

So they left the oldest brother in the midst of his wine and went on farther until they came to a broad field where flocks of pigeons were feeding.

"If I were to grant you one wish," the Angel said to the second brother, "what would you ask?"

"I'd be happy, father, if all the pigeons in this field were turned to sheep and belonged to me."

The Angel lifted his staff, made the sign of the cross, and lo! the field was covered with sheep. Sheds appeared and houses and women, some of them milking the ewes and others skimming the milk and making cheeses. In one place men were busy preparing meat for the market and in another cleaning wool. And all of them as they came and went spoke respectfully to the second brother and called him, "Master!"

"You have your wish," the Angel said. "Stay here and enjoy prosperity and see that you do not forget God's poor!"

Then he and the youngest brother went on their way

"Now, my son," the Angel said, "you, too, may make one wish."

"I want but one thing, father. I pray heaven to grant me a truly pious wife. That is my only wish."

"A truly pious wife!" the Angel cried. "My boy, you have asked the hardest thing of all! Why, there are only three truly pious women in all the world! Two of them are already married and the third is a princess who is being sought in marriage at this very moment by two kings! However, your brothers have received their wishes and you must have yours, too. Let us go at once to the father of this virtuous princess and present your suit."

So just as they were they trudged to the city where the princess lived and presented themselves at the palace looking shabby and travel-stained.

The king received them and when he heard their mission he looked at them in amazement.

"This makes three suitors for my daughter's hand! Two kings and now this young man all on the same day! How am I going to decide among them?"

"Let heaven decide!" the Angel said. "Cut three branches of grape-vine and let the princess mark each branch with the name of a different suitor. Then let

her plant the three branches to-night in the garden and
to-morrow do you give her in marriage to the man whose
branch has blossomed during the night and by morning
is covered with ripe clusters of grapes."

The king and the two other suitors agreed to this and
the princess named and planted three branches of grape-
vine. In the morning two of the branches were bare
and dry, but the third, the one which was marked with
the name of the youngest brother, was covered with
green leaves and ripe clusters of grapes. The king accepted heaven's ruling and at once led his daughter to
church where he had her married to the stranger and
sent her off with his blessing.

The Angel led the young couple to a forest and left
them there.

A year went by and the Angel was sent back to earth
to see how the three brothers were faring. Assuming
the form of an old beggar, he went to the oldest brother
who was busy among his wine-presses and begged the
charity of a cup of wine.

"Be off with you, you old vagabond!" the oldest
brother shouted angrily. "If I gave a cup of wine to
every beggar that comes along I'd soon be a beggar myself!"

The Angel lifted his staff, made the sign of the cross,

and lo! the wine and all the winepresses disappeared
and in their place flowed a broad deep river.

"In your prosperity you have forgotten God's poor,"
the Angel said. "Go back to your pear tree."

Then the Angel went to the second brother who was
busy in his dairy.

"Brother," the Angel said, "in heaven's name, I pray
you, give me a morsel of cheese."

"A morsel of cheese, you lazy good-for-nothing!"
the second brother cried. "Be off with you or I'll call
the dogs!"

The Angel lifted his staff, made the sign of the cross,
and lo! the sheep and the dairy and all the busy laborers
disappeared and he and the second brother were standing there alone in a field where flocks of pigeons were
feeding.

"In your prosperity you have forgotten God's poor,"
the Angel said. "Go back to your pear tree!"

Then the Angel made his way to the forest where he
had left the youngest brother and his wife. He found
them in great poverty living in a mean little hut.

"God be with you!" said the Angel still in the guise
of an old beggar. "I pray you in heaven's name give
me shelter for the night and a bite of supper."

"We are poor ourselves," the youngest brother said.

"But come in, you are welcome to share what we have."

They put the old beggar to rest at the most comfortable place beside the fire and the wife set three places for the evening meal. They were so poor that the loaf that was baking in the oven was not made of grain ground at the mill but of pounded bark gathered from the trees.

"Alas," the wife murmured to herself, "it shames me that we have no real bread to put before our guest."

Imagine then her surprise when she opened the oven and saw a browned loaf of wheaten bread.

"God be praised!" she cried.

She drew a pitcher of water at the spring but when she began pouring it into the cups she found to her joy that it was changed to wine.

"In your happiness," the Angel said, "you have not forgotten God's poor and God will reward you!"

He raised his staff, made the sign of the cross, and lo! the mean little hut disappeared and in its place arose a stately palace full of riches and beautiful things. Servants passed hither and thither and addressed the poor man respectfully as "My lord!" and his wife as "My lady!"

The old beggar arose and as he went he blessed them both, saying:

"God gives you these riches and they will be yours to enjoy so long as you share them with others."

They must have remembered the Angel's words for all their lives long they were happy and prosperous.

THE VILAS' SPRING

*The Story of the Brother Who Knew That Good Was
Stronger Than Evil*

THE VILAS' SPRING

THERE was once a rich man who had two sons.
The older son was overbearing, greedy, and covet-
ous. He was dishonest, too, and thought nothing of taking things that belonged to others. The younger
brother was gentle and kind. He was always ready
to share what he had and he was never known to cheat
or to steal.

"He's little better than a fool!" the older brother
used to say of him scornfully.

When the brothers grew to manhood the old father
died leaving directions that they divide his wealth between them, share and share alike.

"Nonsense!" the older brother said. "That fool
would only squander his inheritance! To every poor
beggar that comes along he'd give an alms until soon
my poor father's savings would be all gone! No! I'll
give him three golden ducats and a horse and tell him
to get out and if he makes a fuss I won't give him that
much!"

So he said to his younger brother:

"You're a fool and you oughtn't to have a penny from our father's estate. However, I'll give you three golden ducats and a horse on condition that you clear out and never come back."

"Brother," the younger one said quietly, "you are doing me a wrong."

"What if I am?" sneered the older. "Wrong is stronger than Right just as I am stronger than you. Be off with you now or I'll take from you even these three golden ducats and the horse!"

Without another word the younger brother mounted the horse and rode away.

Time went by and at last the brothers chanced to meet on the highway.

"God bless you, brother!" the younger one said.

"Don't you go God-blessing me, you fool!" the older one shouted. "It isn't God who is powerful in this world but the Devil!"

"No, brother," the other said, "you are wrong. God is stronger than the Devil just as Good is stronger than Evil."

"Are you sure of that?"

"Yes, brother, I'm sure."

"Well, then, let us make a wager. I'll wager you a golden ducat that Evil is stronger than Good and we'll let the first man we meet on this road decide which of us is right.   Do you agree?"

" Yes, brother, I agree."

They rode a short distance and overtook a man who seemed to be a monk. He wasn't really a monk but the Devil himself disguised in the habit of a monk. The older brother put the case to him and the false monk at once answered:

" That's an easy question to decide. Of course Evil is stronger than Good in this world."

Without a word the younger brother took out one of his golden ducats and handed it over.

" Now," sneered the older one, " are you convinced? "

" No, brother, I am not. No matter what this monk says I know that Good is stronger than Evil."

" You do, do you? Then suppose we repeat the wager and ask the next man we meet to decide between us."

" Very well, brother, I'm willing."

The next man they overtook looked like an old farmer, but in reality he was the Devil again who had taken the guise of a farmer. They put the question to him and of course the Devil made the same answer:

" Evil is stronger than Good in this world."

So again the younger brother paid his wager but insisted that he still believed Good to be stronger than Evil.

"Then we'll make a third wager," the other said.

With the Devil's help the older brother won the third golden ducat which was all the money the younger one had. Then the older brother suggested that they wager their horses and the Devil, disguised in another form, again acted as umpire and the younger one of course lost his horse.

"Now I have nothing more to lose," he said, "but I am still so sure that Good is stronger than Evil that I am willing to wager the very eyes out of my head!"

"The more fool you!" the other one cried brutally.

Without another word he knocked his younger brother down and gouged out his eyes.

"Now let God take care of you if He can! As for me I put my trust in the Devil!"

"May God forgive you for speaking so!" the younger one said.

"I don't care whether He does or not! Nothing can harm me! I'm strong and I'm rich and I know how to take care of myself. As for you, you poor blind beggar, is there anything you would like me to do for you before I ride away?"

"All I ask of you, brother, is that you lead me to

Vilas at Play

the spring that is under the fir tree not far from
here. There I can bathe my wounds and sit in the
shade."

" I'll do that much for you," the older one said, taking the blinded man by the hand. " For the rest, God
will have to take care of you."

With that he led him over to the fir tree and left him.
The blinded man groped his way to the spring and
bathed his wounds, then sat down under the tree and
prayed God for help and protection.

When night came he fell asleep and he slept until
midnight when he was awakened by the sound of voices
at the spring. A company of Vilas were bathing and
playing as they bathed. He was blind, as you remember, so he couldn't see their beautiful forms but he knew
that they must be Vilas from their voices which were
as sweet as gurgling waters and murmuring treetops.
Human voices are never half so lovely. Yes, they must
be Vilas from the mountains and the woods.

" Ho, sisters! " cried one of them, " if only men knew
that we bathed in this spring, they could come to-
morrow and be healed in its water—the maimed and
the halt and blind! To-morrow this water would
heal even the king's daughter who is afflicted with
leprosy! "

When they were gone the blind man crept down to
the spring and bathed his face. At the first touch of
the healing water his wounds closed and his sight was
restored. With a heart full of gratitude he knelt down
and thanked God for the miracle. Then when morning
came he filled a vessel with the precious water and hurried to the king's palace.

" Tell the king," he said to the guards, " that I have
come to heal his daughter."

The king admitted him at once to the princess's chamber and said to him:

" If you succeed in healing the princess you shall have
her in marriage and in addition I shall make you heir
to my kingdom."

The moment the princess was bathed in the healing
water she, too, was restored to health and at once the
proclamation was sent forth that the princess was recovered and was soon to marry the man who had cured
her.

Now when the evil older brother heard who this fortunate man was, he could scarcely contain himself for
rage and envy.

" How did that fool get back his sight?" he asked
himself. " What magic secret did he discover that en-
abled him to heal the princess of leprosy? Whatever it

was he got it under the fir tree for where else could he have got it? I've a good mind to go to the fir tree myself to-night and see what happens."

The more he thought about it the surer he became that if he went to the fir tree in exactly the same condition as his brother he, too, would have some wonderful good fortune. So when night came he seated himself under the tree, gouged out his eyes with a knife, and then waited to see what would happen. At midnight he heard the Vilas at the spring but their voices were not sweet but shrill and angry.

"Sisters," they cried to each other, "have you heard? The princess is healed of leprosy and it was with the water of this, our spring! Who has spied on us?"

"While we were talking last night," said one, "some man may have been hiding under the fir tree."

"Let us see if there is any one there to-night!" cried another.

With that they all rushed to the fir tree and took the man they found sitting there and in a fury tore him to pieces as though he were a bit of old cloth. So that was the end of the wicked older brother. And you will notice that in his hour of need his friend, the Devil, was not on hand to help him.

So after all it was the younger brother who finally inherited all his father's wealth. In addition he married the princess and was made heir to the kingdom. So you see Good is stronger than Evil in this world.

LORD AND MASTER

The Story of the Man Who Understood the Language of the Animals

LORD AND MASTER

THERE was once a young shepherd, an honest industrious fellow, who passed most of his time in the hills looking after his master's flocks. One afternoon he happened upon a bush which some gipsies had set a-fire. As he stopped to watch it he heard a strange hissing, whistling sound. He went as close as he could and in the center of the bush which the flames had not yet reached he saw a snake. It was writhing and trembling in fear.

" Help me, brother! " the snake said. " Help me and I will reward you richly! I swear I will! "

The shepherd put the end of his crook over the flames and the snake crawled up the crook, up the shepherd's arm, and wound itself about his neck.

It was now the shepherd's turn to be frightened.

" What! Will you kill me as a reward for my kindness? "

" Nay," the snake said. " Do not be afraid. I will not injure you. Do as I tell you and you will have nothing to regret. My father is the Tsar of the Snakes.

Take me to him and he will reward you for rescuing me."

" But I can't leave my flocks," the shepherd said.

" Have no fear about your flocks. Nothing will happen to them in your absence."

" But I don't know where your father, the Tsar of the Snakes, lives," the shepherd protested.

" I'll show you," the snake said. " I'll point out the direction with my tail."

So in spite of his misgivings the shepherd at last agreed to the snake's suggestion and, leaving his sheep in God's care, started up the mountainside in the direction which the snake pointed out with his tail.

They reached finally a sort of pocket in the hills which was sandy and rocky and exposed to the full force of the sun. The snake directed the shepherd to the entrance of a cave which had a huge door composed entirely of living snakes closely wound together. The shepherd's snake said something in his breathy whistling voice and the door pulled itself apart and allowed the shepherd to enter the cave.

" Now," whispered the snake, " when my father asks you what you want, tell him you want the gift of understanding the language of the animals. He will try to give you something else but don't you accept anything else."

The Tsar of the Snakes was a huge creature clothed in a gorgeous skin of red and yellow and black. They found him reclining on a golden table with a crown of precious jewels on his head.

" My son! " he cried, when he saw the snake that was still wound about the shepherd's neck, " where have you been? We have been grieving for you thinking you had met some misfortune."

" But for this shepherd, my father," the snake said, " I should have been burned to death. He rescued me."

Then he told the Tsar of the Snakes the whole story. The Tsar of the Snakes listened carefully and when the Snake Prince was finished he turned to the shepherd and said:

" Sir, I am deeply indebted to you for saving my son's life. Ask of me anything I can grant and it is yours."

" Give me then," the shepherd said, " the gift of understanding the language of the animals."

" Not that! " the Tsar of the Snakes cried. " It is too dangerous a gift! If ever you confessed to some other human being that you had this gift and repeated what some animal said you would die that instant. Ask something else—anything else! "

" No," the shepherd insisted. " Give me that or nothing! "

When the Tsar of the Snakes saw that the shepherd was not to be dissuaded, he said:

" Very well, then. What must be, must be. Come now very close to me and put your mouth against my mouth. Do you breathe three times into my mouth and I shall breathe three times into your mouth. Then you will understand the language of the animals."

So the shepherd put his mouth close to the mouth of the Tsar of the Snakes and breathed into it three times. Then the Tsar of the Snakes breathed into the shepherd's mouth three times.

" Now you will understand the language of all animals," the Tsar of the Snakes said. " It is a dangerous gift but if you remember my warning it may bring you great prosperity. Farewell."

So the shepherd went back to his flocks and lay down under a fir tree to rest. Presently he wondered whether he hadn't been asleep and dreamed about the burning bush and the snake and the Tsar of the Snakes.

" It can't be real! " he said to himself. " How can I or any man understand the language of the animals! "

The Tsar of the Snakes Listened Carefully

Just then two ravens alighted on the tree above his head.

"Caw! Caw!" said one of them. "Wouldn't that shepherd be surprised if he knew he was lying on some buried treasure!"

"Caw! Caw!" laughed the other. "He'll never know for he's only one of those poor stupid human beings who can't understand a word we say!"

The ravens flew off and the shepherd sat up and rubbed his eyes to make sure he was awake.

"Am I dreaming again?" he asked himself, "or did I really understand them? Well, I'll soon find out. To-morrow I'll bring a spade and then if there's any treasure buried under this tree I won't be long in digging it up."

He marked the spot where he had been lying when the ravens spoke and the next day came back and dug. Three feet below the surface his spade hit something that proved to be a big iron pot chock-full of golden ducats.

He carried the treasure to his master and his master was so pleased at his honesty that he gave him half of it.

So now the shepherd was able to set up in life for himself. He bought a farm and married and "settled

down " as the saying is.   The years went by and he
grew prosperous and rich.

One Christmas Eve he said to his wife:

" I'm thinking, wife, of my youth when I was a shepherd and how lonely it was at times like this when other
folk were at home seated about the fire and making
merry. Let us give our shepherds out on the hills a surprise to-night. We can take them meats and wine and
other food and then I'll go out and guard the sheep
while you serve them a fine Christmas supper."

His wife agreed and they mounted their horses and
rode out to the hills taking with them great hampers
of food and wine. The wife entertained the shepherds
in their hut with a big jolly supper and the master stayed
outside all night with the dogs guarding the sheep.

At midnight some wolves came prowling around the
flocks.

" See here," they said to the dogs, " if you let us in
we'll kill the sheep and then we'll divide the carcasses
with you."

The dogs for the most part were young and thought-
less and ready enough to fall in with the wolves' suggestion. But there was one old sheepdog that nothing
could tempt.

" I've only a few teeth left! " he growled, " but those

few are still sound and let any wolf come a step nearer
and I'll tear him to pieces! "

All night long that one old sheepdog stood on guard
faithful to duty.

In the morning the master ordered the shepherds to
kill the young dogs and train in new ones.

The shepherds were surprised.

" The master's a clever one! " they told each other.
" Just one night and he found out how worthless those
young dogs were! "

As the farmer and his wife were riding home, the
farmer's horse ran on ahead.

" Not so fast! " begged the mare that the wife was
riding. " Have pity on me and go more slowly. You
have only the master to carry while I'm all laden down
with hampers and empty jugs and I don't know what
and with a mistress that's twice as big as she was a few
months ago! "

The farmer when he heard the mare's complaint burst
out laughing.

" What are you laughing at? " his wife asked sharply.

" Nothing," the farmer said.

" You're laughing at me! " the wife declared, " I
know you are, just because I'm so big that I'm awkward
in the saddle! "

"No, my dear, I'm not laughing at you, truly I'm not."

"You are! I know you are and I don't think it's kind of you, either!" And the wife burst into tears.

"Now, my dear," the husband said, soothingly, "be sensible and believe me when I tell you I was not laughing at you."

"Then what were you laughing at?"

"I can't tell you because if I did tell you then I should die the next moment."

"Die the next moment!" the wife said. "Stuff and nonsense! It must be a strange thing indeed if a man can't tell his own wife for fear he'll die the next moment!"

The more she thought about it the more enraged she became and also the more curious.

"If you really loved me, you'd tell me!" she wept.

All the way home she kept on worrying her husband and nagging at him until at last in utter exhaustion he said:

"Peace, woman, peace, and I'll tell you! But first let me have my coffin made for as I've warned you I shall die the moment I've spoken."

So he had the village carpenter build him a coffin

and when it was ready he stood it up on end against the house and got inside of it.

The news of what was about to happen spread among the animals and the faithful old sheepdog hurried down from the hills to be with his master at the end. He lay down at the foot of the coffin and howled.

" I've one faithful friend! " the farmer said. " Wife, give the poor dog some bread before I tell you my secret and die."

The woman threw the old dog a hunk of bread but the dog refused it and kept on howling.

The rooster from the barnyard came running up and began gobbling down the bread with great gusto.

" You shameless animal! " the dog said sternly. " Here's the poor master about to die on account of that foolish inquisitive wife of his and yet you have so little feeling that you're delighted at the chance to gorge yourself with food! "

The rooster clucked scornfully.

" See here, old dog, I can't waste any sympathy on that master of ours! Any man who allows his wife to bully him deserves whatever he gets! Look at me! " The rooster puffed out his chest and gave a loud: " *Cock-a-doodle-do!* I've got fifty wives but do they bully me? They do not! Whenever I find a nice fat

worm or a grain of corn I set up an awful noise and
gather them all around me. Then I eat it while they
stand there and admire me! No, no, old dog, I have no
patience with the master! He has only one wife and he
doesn't know how to rule her!"

"The rooster's right!" thought the farmer.

With that he jumped out of the coffin, picked up a
stick, and gave his wife a sound beating.

"So you'd kill your husband just to satisfy your
curiosity, would you?" he shouted angrily. "Very
well, then! Take this and this and this! And if your
curiosity is still unsatisfied I'll give you some more!"

"Stop! Stop! Stop!" cried the wife. "Do you
want to injure me!"

But the farmer did not stop until he had given her
such a whipping that she never forgot it. When it was
over she begged his pardon humbly and promised never
again to ask him anything that he didn't want to tell her.

"You just mustn't let me be so foolish again!" she
said.

"I won't!" the farmer declared.

Then he puffed out his chest and strutted about until
you'd have laughed to see him—he looked so much like
the rooster!

THE SILVER TRACKS

The Story of the Poor Man Who Befriended a Beggar

THE SILVER TRACKS

THERE were once three brothers who lived in the same village. One of them was very rich. He had houses and fields and barns. He had nothing to spend his money on for he had no children and his wife was as saving and hardworking as himself. The second brother was not so rich but he, too, was prosperous. He had one son and all his thought was to accumulate money and property in order to leave his son rich. He schemed and worked and slaved and made his wife do the same.

The third brother was industrious but very poor. He worked early and late and never took a holiday. He couldn't afford to for he. had a wife and ten children and only by working every hour of the day and often far into the night could he earn enough to buy food for so large a family. He was a simple man and a good man and he taught his children that the most important thing for them to do in life was to love God and be kind to their fellowmen.

Now it happened that once, when our Lord Christ was on earth testing out the hearts of men, he came in the guise of a beggar to the village where the three brothers lived. He came in a brokendown cart driving a wheezy old horse. It was cold and raining and night was falling.

The Beggar knocked at the door of the richest brother and said:

" I pray you in God's name give shelter for the night to me and my horse."

" What! " cried the rich man, " do you suppose I have nothing better to do than give shelter to such as you! Be off with you or I'll call my men and have them give you the beating you deserve! "

The Beggar left without another word and went to the house of the next brother. He was civil at least to the Beggar and pretended that he was sorry to refuse him.

" I'd accommodate you if I could," he said, " but the truth is I can't. My house isn't as big as it looks and I have many people dependent on me. Just go on a little farther and I'm sure you'll find some one who will take you in."

The Beggar turned his horse's head and went to the tiny little house where the poor brother lived with his big family. He knocked on the door and begged for shelter.

"Come in, brother," said the Poor Man. "We're pretty crowded here but we'll find a place for you."

"And my horse," the Beggar said; "I'm afraid to leave him out in the rain and cold."

"We'll stable him with my donkey," the Poor Man said. "Do you come in here by the fire and dry off and I'll see to the horse."

The Poor Man pulled out his own cart until it was exposed to the rain in order to make a dry place in the shed for the Beggar's cart. Then he led the Beggar's gaunt horse into his tiny stable and fed him for the night out of his own slender store of oats and hay.

He and his family shared their evening meal with the Beggar and then made up for him a bed of straw near the fire where he was able to pass the night comfortably and warmly.

The next morning as he was leaving he said to the Poor Man:

"You must come sometime to my house and visit me and let me return the hospitality you have shown me."

"Where do you live?" the Poor Man asked.

"You can always find me," the Beggar said, "by following the tracks of my cart. You will know them because they are broader than the tracks of any other cart. You will come, won't you?"

"Yes," the Poor Man promised, "I will if ever I have time."

They bade each other good-by and the Beggar drove slowly off. Then the Poor Man went to the shed to get his own cart and the first thing he saw were two large silver bolts lying on the ground.

"They must have fallen from the Beggar's cart!" he thought to himself and he ran out to the road to see whether the Beggar were still in sight. But he and the cart had disappeared.

"I hope he has no accident on account of those bolts!" the Poor Man said.

When he went to the stable to get his donkey he found four golden horse-shoes where the Beggar's horse had been standing.

"Four golden horse-shoes!" he exclaimed. "I ought to return them and the silver bolts at once! But I can't to-day, I'm too busy. Well, I'll hide them safely away and some afternoon when I have a few hours to spare I'll follow the tracks of the cart to the Beggar's house."

That afternoon he met his two rich brothers and told them about the Beggar.

"Silver bolts!" cried one.

"Golden horse-shoes!" cried the other. "Take us home with you and let us see them!"

So they went home with the Poor Man and saw for themselves the silver bolts and the golden horse-shoes.

"Brothers," the Poor Man said, "if either of you have time I wish you'd take these things and return them to the Beggar."

They both said, no, no, they hadn't time, but they would like to know where the Beggar lived.

"He said I could always find him," the Poor Man said, "by following the tracks of his cart."

"The tracks of his cart!" echoed the other two. "Show us the tracks of his cart!"

They went to the shed where the cart had been and followed the tracks out to the road. Even on the road they were easy to see for besides being wider than any other cart tracks they shone white like glistening silver.

"H'm! H'm!" murmured the two rich brothers.

"You don't think either of you have time to follow them to the Beggar's house?" the Poor Man said.

"No! Of course not! Of course not!" they both answered.

But in his heart each had already decided to go at once and see for himself what kind of a Beggar this was who had silver bolts in his cart and golden shoes on his horse.

The oldest brother went the very next day driving a new wagon and a fine horse. The silver tracks led through woods and fields and over hills. They came at last to a river which was spanned by a wooden bridge. It was cunningly constructed of timbers beautifully hewn. The rich man had never seen such wood used on a bridge.

By the roadside beyond the bridge there was a pigsty with one trough full of corn and another full of water. There were two sows in the sty and they were fighting each other and tearing at each other and paying no attention whatever to all the good food in the trough.

A little farther on there was another river and over it another wonderful bridge, this one made entirely of stone.

Beyond it the rich man came to a meadow where there was a hayrick around which two angry bulls were chasing each other and goring each other until the blood spurted.

"I wonder some one doesn't stop them!" the rich man thought to himself.

The next river had an iron bridge, more beautiful than

the rich man had ever supposed an iron bridge could be.

Beyond the iron bridge there was a field and a bush and two angry rams that were chasing each other around the bush and fighting. Their horns cracked as they met and their hides were torn and bleeding where they had gored each other.

" I never saw so many angry fighting animals! " the rich man thought to himself.

The next bridge glowed in the sun like the embers of a fire for it was built entirely of shining copper—copper rivets, copper plates, copper beams, nothing but copper.

The silver tracks led over the copper bridge into a broad valley. By the roadside there was a high crossbar from which depended heavy cuts of meat—lamb and pork and veal. Two large bitch dogs were jumping at the meat and then snarling and snapping at each other.

The next bridge was the loveliest of them all for it was built of white gleaming silver.

The rich man climbed down from his wagon and examined it closely.

" It would be worth a man's while to carry home a piece of this bridge! " he muttered to himself.

He tried the rivets, he shook the railing. At last he found four loose bolts which he was able to pull out.

The four together were so heavy that he was scarcely able to lift them. He looked cautiously about and when he saw that no one was looking, he slipped them one by one into the bottom of his wagon and covered them with straw. Then he turned his horse's head and drove home as fast as he could. It was midnight when he got there and nobody about to spy on him as he hid the silver bolts in the hay.

The next day when he went out alone to gloat over his treasure he found instead of four heavy silver bolts four pieces of wood!

So that's what the rich brother got for following the silver tracks.

A day or two later without saying a word to any one, the second brother decided that he would follow the silver tracks and have a look at the strange Beggar whose cart had silver bolts and whose wheezy horse had golden shoes.

"Perhaps if I keep my wits about me I'll be able to pick up a few golden horse-shoes. Not many boys inherit golden horse-shoes from their fathers!"

Well, the second brother went over exactly the same route and saw exactly the same things. He crossed all those wonderful bridges that his brother had crossed— the wooden bridge, the stone bridge, the iron bridge,

The Beggar's Garden

the copper bridge, the silver bridge, and he saw all those angry animals still trying to gore each other to death.

He didn't stop at the silver bridge for he thought to himself:

" Perhaps the next bridge will be golden and if it is I may be able to break off a piece of it! "

Beyond the silver bridge was another broad valley and the second brother saw many strange sights as he drove through. There was a man standing alone in a field and trying to beat off a flock of ravens that were swooping down and pecking at his eyes. Near him was an old man with snow-white hair who was making loud outcries to heaven praying to be delivered from the two oxen who were munching at his white hair as though it were so much hay. They ate great wisps of it and the more they ate the more grew out.

There was an apple-tree heavily laden with ripe fruit and a hungry man forever reaching up and plucking an apple. The apples were apples of Sodom and always as the hungry man raised each new one to his mouth it turned to ashes.

In another place a thirsty man was reaching with a dipper into a well and always, just as he was about to scoop up some water, the well moved away from under the dipper.

"What a strange country this is!" thought the second brother as he drove on.

At last he reached the next bridge and sure enough it was shining gold! Every part of it—bolts and beams and pillars, all were gold. In great excitement the second brother climbed down from his wagon and began pulling and wrenching at various parts of the bridge hoping to find some loose pieces which he could break off. At last he succeeded in pulling out four long bolts which were so heavy he could scarcely lift them. After looking about in all directions to make sure that no one saw him, he put them into his wagon and covered them up with straw. Then he drove homewards as fast as he could.

"Ha! Ha!" he chuckled as he hid the golden bolts in the barn. "My son will now be a richer man than my brother!"

He could scarcely sleep with thinking of his golden treasure and at the first light of morning he slipped out to the barn. Imagine his rage when he found in the straw four bolts of wood!

So that was all the second brother got for following the silver tracks.

Well, years went by and the Poor Man worked day after day and all day and often far into the night. Some

of his children died and the rest grew up and went out
into the world and married and made homes of their
own. Then at last his good wife died and the time came
when the Poor Man was old and all alone in the world.

One night as he sat on his doorstep thinking of his
wife and of his children when they were little and of all
the years he had worked for them to keep them fed and
clothed, he happened to remember the Beggar and the
promise he had made to visit him sometime.

"And to think of all the years I've kept his golden
horse-shoes and his silver bolts! Well, he'll forgive me,
I know," thought the Poor Man, "for he'll understand
that I've always been too busy up to this time ever to
follow the tracks of his cart. I wonder are they still
there."

He went out to the roadside and peered down and how
it happened I don't know, but to his dim eyes at least
there were the silver tracks as clear as ever.

"Good!" cried the Poor Man. "To-morrow morning bright and early I'll hitch up the donkey and visit
my old friend, the Beggar!"

So the next day he took out the silver bolts and the
golden horseshoes from the place where he had kept
them hidden all these years and he put them in a bag.
Then he hitched his old donkey to his old cart and

started out to follow the silver tracks to the Beggar's home.

Well, he saw just exactly the same things that his brothers had seen those many years before: all those terrible fighting animals and all those unfortunate men.

"I'll have to remember and ask the Beggar what ails all these creatures," he thought to himself.

Like his brothers he passed over the wooden bridge and the stone bridge and the iron bridge and the copper bridge and the silver bridge and even the golden bridge. Beyond the golden bridge he came to a Garden that was surrounded by a high wall of diamonds and rubies and sapphires and all kinds of precious stones that blazed as brightly as the sun itself. The silver tracks turned in at the garden gate which was locked.

The poor man climbed down from his cart, unhitched the donkey, and set him out to graze on the tender grass that grew by the wayside.

Then he took the bag that held the golden horse-shoes and the silver bolts and he went to the garden gate. It was a very wonderful gate of beaten gold set with precious stones. For a moment the Poor Man wondered if he dare knock at so rich a gate, then he remembered that his friend the Beggar was inside and he knew that he would be made welcome.

It was the Beggar himself who opened the gate. When he saw the Poor Man he smiled and held out his hands and said:

"Welcome, dear friend! I have been waiting for you all these years! Come in and I will show you my Garden."

So the Poor Man went inside. And first of all he gave the Beggar his golden horse-shoes and his silver bolts.

"Forgive me," he said, "for keeping them so long, but I've never had time until now to return them."

The Beggar smiled.

"I knew, dear friend, that they were safe with you and that you would bring them some day."

Then the Beggar put his arm over the Poor Man's shoulder and led him through the Garden showing him the wonderful golden fruits and beautiful flowers. They sat them down beside a fountain of crystal water and while they listened to the songs of glorious birds they talked together and the Poor Man asked about the strange things he had seen along the road.

"All those animals," the Beggar said, "were once human beings who instead of fearing God and being kind to their fellowmen passed all their time fighting and cheating and cursing. The two sows were two sisters-

in-law who hated each other bitterly. The two bulls
and the two rams were neighbors who fought for years
and years over the boundary lines of their farms and
now they keep on fighting through eternity. The two
bitches were two sisters who fought until they died over
the inheritance left them by their father. The old man
whose hair the oxen eat was a farmer who always pas-
tured his cattle on his neighbors' fields. Now he has
his reward. The man at whose eyes the ravens peck
was an ungrateful son who mistreated his parents. The
man with the awful thirst that can never be quenched
was a drunkard, and the one at whose lips the apples
turn to ashes was a glutton."

So they talked on together, the Poor Man and the
Beggar, until it was late afternoon and the Beggar said:

"And now, dear friend, you will sup with me as I
once supped with you."

"Thank you," the Poor Man said, "I will. But let
me first go out and see how my donkey is."

"Very well," the Beggar said, "go. But be sure to
come back for I shall be waiting for you."

So the Poor Man went out the garden gate and
looked for his donkey. But the donkey was gone.

"He must have started home," the Poor Man
thought. "I'll hurry and overtake him."

So he started back afoot the way he had come. He
went on and on but saw no donkey. He crossed the
golden bridge and the silver bridge and the copper
bridge and the iron bridge and the stone bridge and
last of all the wooden bridge, but still there was no donkey.

"He must have got all the way home," he thought.

When the Poor Man reached his native village things
looked different. Houses that he remembered had disappeared and others had taken their places. He couldn't
find his own little house at all. He asked the people
he met and they knew nothing about it. And they knew
nothing about him, either, not even his name. And nobody even knew about his sons. At last he did meet
one old man who remembered the family name and
who told him that many years before the last of the sons
had gone to another village to live.

"There's no place here for me," the Poor Man
thought. "I better go back to my friend the Beggar
and stay with him. No one else wants me."

So once again he followed the silver tracks all that
long way over all those bridges and when at last he
reached the garden gate he was very tired, for he was
old and feeble now. It was all he could do to give one
faint little knock. But the Beggar heard him and came

running to let him in.   And when he saw him, how tired
he was and how feeble, he put his arm around him and
helped him into the Garden and he said:

"You shall stay with me now forever and we shall
be very happy together."

And the Poor Man when he looked in the Beggar's
face to thank him saw that he was not a beggar at all
but the Blessed Christ Himself.   And then he knew
that he was in the Garden of Paradise.

THE END